M... ...veway, tired
and ...ppy from her day with Josh ...t the beach.
But when she saw who was standing by her
front door, she stiffened, feeling as if she'd
been doused with a bucket of ice water.

"Hi, Monica. Did you get the message that I
called?" Warren asked, stepping down from
the doorway, where he'd been standing with
her mother. In his pleated beige slacks and
argyle cotton sweater, he looked like a fashion
model.

"Huh? Oh—yes."

At that moment, Josh appeared from behind
the van. His tee-shirt was bunched up on one
side, and his curly hair was an unruly mop.
"Hi, I'm Josh Ross," he said easily.

Warren took a possessive step toward
Monica. Draping his arm around her, he gave
Josh a jealous glare. Josh shifted, clearly
picking up on the unspoken message.

Monica looked at her mother's face, and all
the good feelings from her afternoon with Josh
disappeared. Obviously she was being asked
whose side she was on, but she didn't know
what to do. There was a pounding in her head,
and she felt as if she were being pulled apart.

Suddenly, she couldn't take it anymore.

SUNSET HIGH

A CHANCE TO MAKE IT

Linda A. Cooney

FAWCETT GIRLS ONLY • NEW YORK

RLI:

VL: Grades 6 + up

IL: Grades 7 + up

A Fawcett Girls Only Book
Published by Ballantine Books
Copyright © 1985 by Kevin Cooney, Linda Alper and the
Cloverdale Press, Inc.

Library of Congress Catalog Card Number: 85-91239

ISBN 0-449-12879-2

Manufactured in the United States of America

First Edition: January 1986

❀ 1

MONICA MILLER WHIPPED OFF HER SWEATSHIRT, TOSSED IT onto the bed, and frowned. It was the seventh time she'd changed her clothes that morning and she knew she could easily change them a hundred more times. When she felt like this, nothing looked right.

"Yuck," Monica said a few minutes later as she examined herself in the mirror. "There's no way that's what they want!" Off flew the dark cotton sundress that her mom had bought her at a recent Rodeo Drive sale. Instead, she tugged on an old favorite, a pair of pink baggy overalls from Camp Beverly Hills.

"Slightly bozo-ish, but I probably don't have a chance anyway." Monica scrunched her pretty face into a comic mask. One more glance and she paced back across her sunny bedroom to grab her diary off the desk. She had to check it one more time.

May 10: 4:00—audition for television movie

of the week called "Off Balance." 4467 Melrose Avenue—Part of Diana, sixteen-year-old daughter of Tom Selleck. Normal teenager. Wants to get her parents to see her as an independent person.

"A normal teenager?" Monica had to laugh.

Having spent all of her seventeen years in Beverly Hills, California, Monica wasn't so sure she knew what a "normal teenager" was. But if that's what they would be searching for at her afternoon acting audition, she'd do everything she could to look the part.

She retied the straps of her overalls, pinned a plastic palm tree pin to the neckline of her oversized tee-shirt, and blew her dark whispy bangs out of her eyes. Then she shook her head.

"Forget it Miller. You'll never pass."

But it would have to do. One more change and she'd be late for school.

"Normal is about the last thing I am," Monica mumbled as she gathered her math homework and checked her Mickey Mouse watch.

Ever since she'd begun to pursue her acting career again, not much in her life had seemed normal. There was no time for school clubs or talking for hours on the phone. When she was a kid starring on "The Twain Family," she'd thought it was great that she was too busy for Brownie meetings or sleepovers. But now that she was a high school junior and no longer a tv star, Monica felt a strange tugging inside when she saw other kids rush off to dates. She'd turned down so many parties and Saturdays at the mall that most of her old friends had stopped asking.

As Monica opened her desk drawer she realized that in one way it was a relief not to get together with a gang of girls. Getting together with friends meant going over who liked which guy and discussing whether he liked you back. When those conversations came up, Monica didn't have much to contribute. She'd never been really close to a boy. Of course, her mom always told Monica that her career was much more important and that she shouldn't worry because guys only let you down. Maybe that was true. At least Monica tried to tell herself that it was. But why then did she get that empty feeling inside so often? Why couldn't she stop thinking that turning seventeen had to be more than auditions and acting classes and figuring how to be what everybody else was looking for.

"Don't think about this," she whispered, "just concentrate on your career." She lifted her picture and resume from the neat stack inside her desk drawer. Monica paused to stare at it.

This was what Monica Miller was now. A black and white smiling photo. Under her dimpled grin was the label for Rosalind Miller Limited, the theatrical agency owned by her mother. On the other side was her resume, the list of her professional credits. Monica read it over. The long running tv series, "The Twain Family." After that, not much. A chewing gum commercial. A one line movie role. Not much.

"Another audition. Don't blow it," she told the

wide eyed face on the photograph. "Don't let Monica Miller get rejected for the zillionth time."

She pushed back her dark layered hair and took a deep breath. No time to worry about being normal. No time to wish there was something more in her life. All she could think about now was the audition. Maybe today would be different. Maybe today she would be just what they wanted. Slipping her resume into her notebook Monica went down the hall to drop her books and cut back through the living room out to the backyard.

The sun was already strong and Monica squinted when she stepped out. Although there was a light layer of smog, the base of the mountains was still visible off in the distance, and the orange trees gave off a flowery, sweet smell. As Monica sat down at the white metal table next to the swimming pool, she could hear the *flick, flick, flick* of the side lawn sprinklers and the *whoof* of a gardener's leaf blower somewhere out near the street.

"Hi Rosa," Monica called to the maid.

Rosa broke into a smile as she opened the sliding glass door and held out an invitingly full breakfast tray. This patio breakfast was a special treat, since she didn't come every day.

"Good morning," Rosa said. She was about forty years old with thick dark hair and wide Mexican features. As she placed the tray on the table she patted Monica's shoulder. "Your mother ... she wants to talk to you about something important."

"She does?" Monica leaned back in the director's chair and spotted her mother through the glass doors. Mrs. Miller was in the den talking on the telephone at her large modern desk. When she saw Monica she held up a finger in an I'll-be-there-in-one-minute gesture. Then she turned her back and began writing madly. Something was up. Monica felt it. She had to know what it was.

"Thanks." Monica downed the fresh squeezed orange juice and made herself start on her toast and granola. But as soon as she heard the glass door swoosh open she lost interest in breakfast. Her mother was rushing out, looking excited.

"Morning sweetheart. Have I got news for you!" Mrs. Miller was tall and slender with coifed brown hair and a handsome, strong face. As she spoke, she set down a large appointment book and clipped on a pair of pearl earrings.

Monica tensed, her eyes huge. "What is it?" She prayed it was good news about her acting career. Still she held her breath and told herself not to expect anything. She didn't want to be disappointed. Not again.

Mrs. Miller sat down across from her daughter, hanging the jacket of her linen suit over the back of her chair. "That was the Daniels's production office on the phone."

Monica's throat suddenly felt as taut as a bow string. Nervously, she tapped her feet together. Steven Daniels was a very important television executive who was doing a new TV series called "Laurie and Me." It was about a divorced politician mom and her teenage daughter. Monica had auditioned for the daughter's role the week before and the audition had gone well. Being the daughter of a successful single mom, Monica had no trouble relating to the part. She'd known just what they'd wanted.

"What did they say?" Monica was sitting so far forward in her chair that it almost tipped out from under her.

Mrs. Miller waved for Rosa. "Steven's assistant wanted me to know that they loved you. They're very interested in you for the role."

Monica jumped up and the chair clanged back. "They are? I mean, what did they say? Do you think I'll get it? Oh, Mom, that's great!"

"Let's not uncork the champagne yet," Mrs. Miller cautioned. "You know how these things can be."

Monica forced herself to sit down again. Her mother was right. She knew there was a big difference between them being "very interested" and her actually getting the job. Still, this wasn't a one liner or a chewing gum commercial: it was a starring role in a weekly television series!

"They simply said that you did a wonderful audition," Mrs. Miller explained, "and that you are being strongly considered. They don't plan to make a decision for a couple of weeks. But I must say Monica ..." her mom's voice was clear and pointed, "I think we're at a turning point in your career."

"Really?"

"This TV series could be the break we've been waiting for. They're still considering two other girls, but I think you have a good chance."

"Do they want me to audition again?"

Mrs. Miller shook her head. "They're through

auditioning, but I think we still need to do something else if you're going to get this part. I've
decided we should start approaching your career
a little differently." Mrs. Miller paused as Rosa
poured her a cup of coffee.

Monica leaned on her elbows, giving her mother
all her attention. When her mom got that serious
look, Monica knew she meant business. She admired her mother's intelligence and determination. It wasn't every woman who could have
single-handedly transformed herself from an aban-
doned wife with a tiny baby to one of the most
successful agents in Hollywood. Monica often wondered if she needed to be more like her.

"What do you mean Mom?"

"I just mean that you have to start doing whatever you can to help yourself." Mrs. Miller slipped
on a pair of glasses and opened her leather bound
appointment calendar. "Honey, you go to school
with the children of half the people who run this
town. It would be a big help if you got to be
friends with some of them. They're very good
contacts."

Monica felt that strange tugging feeling again,
and she shifted uneasily in her chair. Sunset High
was the main high school for all of Beverly Hills,
and many of her classmates' parents were pro-
ducers or movie executives. Monica's mother had
talked about this before. She called the sons and
daughters of important people "contacts." Monica hated the term "contacts", but she clenched
her hands and made herself listen with an open
mind.

"Like who?" Monica asked, her voice low.

"To start with how about Denis, Steven Daniels's son?"

"Denis?" Ugh. Denis was also a junior at Sunset High, but even if his father was the one who'd decide whether or not she got the role in "Laurie and Me," Monica couldn't imagine becoming close friends with him. Denis Daniels was a good example of the kind of non-normal kid Monica never wanted to become. It was weird how her acting career seemed to keep her from the kids she liked and throw her in with the kids she didn't.

"Mom," Monica objected, "Denis is a total mess. He was suspended from school twice last month. Once for drugs and once for pulling a prank at the Spring dance."

Her mother slipped off her glasses. "What? Denis Daniels? Steven and Deann's son?"

Monica nodded. "Yes, Mom; Denis has wrecked everything he's ever done. He gets away with stuff sometimes because he's so handsome and his mom is a TV star and his dad is a big deal. But Denis really has problems."

Mrs. Miller looked shocked. "I don't believe it. To hear his parents talk about him you'd think he was the perfect all-American boy."

"His parents know what a mess he is."

"Well," Mrs. Miller leaned forward, "when you talk to Mr. Daniels, don't you dare mention anything about Denis's problems. Obviously his parents go to great lengths to make sure that nobody finds out what's really going on."

Monica sighed. "Okay. I don't know when I'd talk to Mr. Daniels about stuff like that anyway ..."

"That's just what I wanted to speak to you about," her mother interrupted. Now her voice was one hundred percent business. She looked down at her appointment book. "There's a party the Saturday after next at the Lawrences'."

Monica cringed. George Lawrence was a famous movie producer and his daughter Nadia also went to Sunset. Nadia was gorgeous, socially powerful, and someone else that Monica preferred to avoid.

"Mr. Daniels will be there," her mother continued. "I want you to go with me and talk to him. It's a perfect chance to see him again and show him that you're just who he's looking for to do that part in 'Laurie and Me.'"

"How am I supposed to do that?" Monica burst out. She couldn't help it. She hated adult Hollywood parties. What was she supposed to do anyway ... walk up to Mr. and Mrs. Daniels and start chatting about the weather, or make up lies about their wonderful son, her classmate?

Mrs. Miller continued. "I want you to ask some very handsome boy to go with you, buy a terrific new dress, and really wow Mr. Daniels."

The tug-o-war inside was getting worse. "Is Nadia going to be there?"

"I would imagine that Nadia will be there. Monica, it wouldn't hurt you to be friendly to Nadia either. Her father just produced an Academy Award winning movie."

Monica tried to eat a spoonful of her now soggy

granola, but her appetite had disappeared. Nadia had never really done anything to hurt her, but the producer's daughter had been really nasty to Monica's new friend, Kristin Sullivan. How could she explain all that to her mom? Kristin was a great person—funny, practical, open. She was Monica's closest friend right now and Monica really liked her. But Kristin had just moved from Minnesota and her father was a doctor—no help at all in the business. Monica wondered if her mother would think Kristin was even worth her loyalty. Certainly Kristin was not a "contact."

Monica watched as Mrs. Miller checked her watch and slipped on her linen jacket.

"By the way," her mother remembered, "how are you doing in advanced biology?"

"About the same." Sunset was a hard school academically and Monica had been having trouble in the science class ever since she'd missed a few days to shoot her commercial.

Her mom quickly downed the rest of her coffee. "I want that grade picked up immediately," she told her daughter. "If you do end up getting the part in 'Laurie and Me,' you don't want a bad grade to stand in your way."

"I know." The juvenile performer's code required that Monica keep her grades high in order to be allowed to work in movies or television. Her mom was right. She had to do something right away to pull up her biology grade.

Finally Mrs. Miller pushed back her chair and stood up. "Well Monica," she challenged, "what do you want to do? Do you want to go for this part or not? Are you serious about your career or aren't you?"

"But Mom, just to go to a party to kiss up to somebody because of a part seems really dishonest. It's like using people."

"Honey, that's the only way to make it. I've been in this business for a long time. I think I know what it takes to succeed."

Monica looked at her mother standing so straight and tall in her tailored beige suit. Her ambition and experience showed in her proud posture. Maybe her mom was right. There was no point in doing things halfway. If she was going to give up friends and guys, she should at least get a successful career in return. And success demanded more than just showing up at auditions. If she went to that party and charmed Mr. Daniels it would definitely increase her chances of getting the role. It was the only way. It was. Monica lifted her head and swallowed hard. "When is the Lawrences' party?"

Mrs. Miller winked approvingly. "A week from Saturday." She closed her appointment book and gathered it under her arm. "That's my girl. I knew my daughter would understand." She gave Monica a little hug. "I've got to go. Call me at the office after you audition for that Tom Selleck thing today and let me know what happened. 'Bye sweetheart."

" 'Bye." Monica watched her mom disappear into the garage before going back in the house to pick up her notebook. The stack was on the kitchen table next to a container of yogurt and some cookies Rosa had left for her. Monica gathered her lunch and her books.

A corner of her photo and resume was sticking out of her notebook and Monica opened the binder to stow the photo more neatly. She was going to take the photo out for one last look, but on second thought she didn't want to see that smiling face right now.

"Monica Miller," she said aloud, "is going to do whatever it takes to make it." Monica clenched her notebook against her chest and closed her eyes.

Whatever it takes. She only prayed it would be worth it.

2

"MAKE SURE THAT YOUR FRIENDS UNDERSTAND THAT SUNSET High is one hip school. Just today we had an arrest, two pregnancies, and an attempted murder."

Kristin Sullivan grabbed the letter she was writing and guarded it against her chest. "What?"

Eddie Santiago, who had been peering over her shoulder, plopped down next to her on the Sunset lawn and grinned. The comedian of the senior class, Eddie was an old friend of her boyfriend, Grady.

"That's right. And tomorrow there's going to be a robbery and someone's going to inherit a million dollars."

Kristin started to laugh. "Sounds serious." She realized that Eddie was referring to the latest project of Ms. Duke's media class—a homemade soap opera. Of all the special courses offered at the wealthy Beverly Hills high school, media class was considered the most exciting. The students had their own TV station, KSUN, and were always working on TV and video projects. Kristin had

13

danced in the last big project—a rock video directed by Grady.

"I don't think I'll make it to graduation at this rate." Eddie leaned over and tried to peek at her letter. "Did you write anything about me?"

Kristin teasingly slid the half-finished letter into her history book. It was to Amy Parker, her best friend back in St. Cloud, Minnesota, where she had lived before moving to Beverly Hills six weeks ago.

"Of couse, I wrote that you were the funniest guy in the senior class, a truly creative dresser, and that you have never seen snow."

Eddie's dark eyes lit up and he brought his bony hands together. Of Chicano origin, he had lived in East Los Angeles until about five years ago, when his parents had made a fortune in the furniture business and moved to Beverly Hills. "Really! You wrote about *moi*?"

"I'd let you read, but you'd get much too embarrassed," she enticed.

"Yeah?"

Kristin laughed, securing her straw "boater" hat with her hand. Her pale, freckled skin wasn't used to the strong California sun, and she hoped to protect her already terminally peeling nose. "Who knows, maybe Amy will be dying to meet you."

"You think so?" Eddie put a hand over his heart, pointing out the latest in a long line of unique fashion statements. It was what he called his "under-designed designer polo shirt." Eddie had stuck a Band-Aid over the designer emblem.

"You never can tell."

Kristin patted Eddie, rearranged her soft cotton skirt, and looked back up the grassy slope for Grady. They'd planned to meet after school. But classes had been out for fifteen minutes, the front lawn was almost deserted, and Grady had not appeared. Kristin stood up to get a better view, feeling the warm breeze toss her long light-brown hair.

"Is Grady still over in the media room?"

Eddie looked around. "I think I saw him leave. We all have to be back there pretty soon to work on the soap. I'm on my way to get some dough-nuts." Eddie suddenly pointed his long arm over toward the tennis courts. "Is that the man him-self?" he asked.

Kristin looked across the lawn and saw a seated figure on the concrete steps just next to the school courts. She immediately recognized Grady's straight, dark hair, long legs, and wide shoulders. But his posture was so listless, so unlike his normal ener-getic self, that for a moment Kristin wasn't sure if it was really Grady. "Is something wrong?" she asked Eddie.

Eddie shrugged. "I don't know. He was acting funky all through class. I tried some of my worst jokes on him, and he didn't even tell me to shut up. Maybe you can figure out what's going on." Eddie waved. "I gotta go. 'Bye."

Kristin picked up her books, and walked slowly across the lawn. As she got closer to the tennis courts she saw that Grady was sitting on the steps, leaning over his folded hands. He wore jeans and the funny multipocketed vest he used for storing tools and lenses when he worked on a media class project. Grady was usually so enthusiastic—so playful and full of life—that Kristin began to worry that something had gone seriously wrong. She quickened her step, walked past the bustle and pop of the tennis courts and around to the stairway.

Once she rounded the corner, Kristin saw that Grady was not alone. Standing a few steps down was Joshua Ross. Josh was a junior, like her, and another close friend of Grady's. The two guys were in the midst of an intense conversation. When Grady saw her he smiled sadly and the conversation ceased.

"Hi there," Kristin said, her voice questioning. She took off her hat and slipped onto the step next to Grady. He put his arm around her. His eyes looked troubled. "Hi, Josh," she said, looking up.

Josh gave her a frustrated smile. He ran his hand through his curly hair and shifted his strong shoulders. Tan and good-looking, he wore clear plastic glasses that gave him a hip, intelligent look. Hooked to his belt was a Walkman.

"I'm glad you're here. This guy's acting like one of our soap opera characters. I want to run and get some juice before we have to be back in the TV studio." Josh looked back at Grady. "You want me to get you anything?"

Grady shook his head. "No, thanks."

Josh backed up and put his headphones over his ears. "I've been trying to tell him he's making too big a deal out of this," he told Kristin. "Maybe he'll listen to you." Josh was earthy and thoughtful, a different temperament entirely from impulsive, wildly imaginative Grady.

"That'll be the day," Kristin replied, smiling.

"Well, I'm going to go fuel up so we can tape the next episode of 'Sunset Dreams.'" That was the name the class had given the soap opera. "We're trying to figure out how to end it. I thought we should have an earthquake."

Grady managed a smile. "Maybe a tidal wave. We could shoot it in the swimming pool."

"How about a volcano? I guess not. Anyway, see you later." Josh pushed the button to start his tape player and jogged down to the street.

After Josh left, Kristin slid closer to Grady. She took his hands and made him look at her. "What's going on?"

Grady shrugged moodily. "Josh is probably right. I'm making too big a deal out of it—but he doesn't know how it feels. He's still got another year at this place. So do you. I feel as if the real world is staring me in the face all of a sudden—and it's scary."

Kristin was baffled ... and concerned. In the beginning of their relationship she had been the troubled one, trying desperately to adjust to a radically new lifestyle. She had struggled to find a way to stay true to herself and yet fit in at Sunset High, while Grady had been the confident, passionate ally. Beverly Hills was his home turf, and he had helped her figure things out. Now it seemed the situation was reversed. Suddenly he looked lost, and she was the secure one.

"Grady, what are you talking about?"

Grady hesitated. "You know Karen Small?"

"Sure." Karen Small was Sunset's student body president, but Kristin couldn't figure out how Karen could have upset him so much. There was a pause as Grady looked off toward the tennis courts. He wore a spacy look on his handsome face, and Kristin finally grew impatient.

"Hello." She snapped her fingers and then gave Grady a gentle nudge with her shoulder. "Are you there?"

Grady blinked and then turned slightly red. "Oh, sorry."

"What about Karen Small?"

"Karen was on the waiting list for Brown...." His voice trailed off.

"And?"

"I just found out that she got her acceptance a couple of days ago."

Kristin took a deep breath. At last she understood. Grady had decided that Yale University was the place he wanted to go as an undergraduate before returning to Los Angeles in four years for film school. He was on the Yale waiting list for acceptance and had been growing more and more worried during the last couple of weeks that he wouldn't get in. Kristin understood now hearing that Karen had been accepted at Brown—another Eastern ivy league college—must have made Grady panicky.

"If you don't get into Yale, you'll stay here and

go to UCLA. There's nothing wrong with that," Kristin reassured him, running her hand along his back.

"I know, but it's the uncertainty that's getting to me. I just feel as if my life here is ending in another month and I have no idea what's going to come next. You don't know how scary that can be."

Kristin looked him straight in the eye. "Don't tell me I don't know how scary change is," she challenged.

That comment caused Grady to smile. He couldn't deny the truth of her statement. After moving halfway across the country to start a new school midsemester, in a strange new place, Kristin had managed to survive—with the help of her new friends. Grady would have to do the same.

"I'm acting like a jerk, right?"

"Right."

Grady gave her a teasing jab with his elbow. "Hey, you don't have to agree with me...."

"You said it first."

Grady paused, falling into his doldrums again. "I don't know. I'm going to be eighteen in two weeks and I'm graduating and I should be really glad."

Kristin smiled. "It's better than being twenty-one and flunking for the third time."

"Somehow that doesn't cheer me up."

"Sorry."

"Well, I guess I just feel ... I don't know ... scared. I'm used to being a big deal here at Sunset and getting to do all that stuff with the media class and then I'll graduate and who knows what will happen."

Kristin gently brushed Grady's hair behind his ear. "It's dumb to worry about this when there's nothing you can do. They'll either accept you or they won't...."

Grady nodded dully.

"I know what!" Kristin decided. "How about if we do a huge party for your eighteenth birthday? We can have a contest to see who can take the best picture of something weird in L.A." She looked over at Grady to see his response. He had an eccentric hobby of photographing L.A. monuments like the huge hot dog statue on top of a stand on La Cienaga Boulevard.

Grady put his head in his hands. "No, thanks."

"Okay," Kristin said, her mind racing. "How about if you take me to two ballet concerts in one day? At least one of us would have a good time."

Grady rolled his eyes. "I just want to ignore the whole thing. I'm just going to study for finals all next weekend."

Kristin was astounded. "Grady, come on. This is ridiculous. We should at least do something for your birthday. It doesn't have to be a party, but we should make it a special occasion."

Grady slowly stood up, his shirttails hanging loosely over his narrow hips. "I don't want to even think about my birthday," he replied grumpily. "We should both just study the whole weekend and forget about it. I'm sorry I'm being such a drag," he added, rubbing his temple. "I'll come out of it soon."

"Promise?"

"Promise."

"Grady, don't worry."

"Okay."

They stood up and he kissed her lightly on the mouth.

Just then Eddie's playful voice boomed from across the lawn. He was bounding over, carrying a white paper sack of doughnuts. Josh ran just ahead of him, holding two plastic containers of brightly colored juice.

"Boys and girls," Eddie called, "I bring delicacies from the far east."

"That's right," laughed Josh, "two blocks over, on Beverly Drive."

"You got it." Eddie tossed a doughnut, and Josh jumped up to catch it. Eddie made a mock pass with another doughnut to Grady, but his friend didn't respond. Grady's two pals looked at Kristin as they came closer, and she shrugged.

Eddie put his arm around Grady. "Why don't I take you back to the studio." He looked back at Kristin as he started to push Grady gently up the stairs. "Maybe fondling a camera will cheer him up."

Grady turned back to his girlfriend. "I'll call you tonight."

"Okay." Kristin folded her arms and watched the two boys disappear into the stucco classroom at the top of the steps. For a moment she just stood there, listening to the nearby tennis game and thinking.

"Want some gazpacho?" Josh asked after the

pause. He was swigging down the orange liquid and handed the jug to Kristin.

She took a gulp. The fresh tomato-cucumber mixture was cool and delicious. "This is good," she told Josh, surprised.

"Mmm," he agreed. His rugged face looked thoughtful and full of purpose. "I may not be a senior, but I know there are more important things than getting into Yale."

Kristin smiled. "I agree. Grady's just really scared all of a sudden."

"Yeah. We should do something to take his mind off it."

They stood a little while longer looking up the concrete staircase. Suddenly a light went on in Kristin's head. "Josh ..." she began excitedly.

He turned to her attentively.

"What if we threw a surprise party for Grady's eighteenth birthday. What do you think of that?"

Josh's handsome face crinkled into a broad smile. "I think that's a great idea! I bet we could even have it at my house."

"Really?"

"I could find out tonight and let you know soon."

"That'd be perfect."

Josh lowered his voice. "We'd have to make sure it stayed a secret, though. We'd have to really make Grady think we're all going to ignore his birthday ... just study all weekend, whatever. He can't find out about it."

"I'll organize it."

"Okay. I think it's a great idea!"

"Me too."

Josh started to head back up to the media room, but turned back as if he'd just remembered something. He cleared his throat. "Maybe Monica could help too." His voice sounded just a little strained all of a sudden.

"I'm sure she would."

Josh stood there for a moment as if he had something else to say, but wasn't sure quite how to say it. "Monica kind of ran out right after school today. Did she have another audition?"

"Yeah. For a movie with Tom Selleck."

"Oh. I thought maybe she was meeting somebody, you know, maybe seeing somebody from a different school or something."

"No"—Kristin paused—"not that I know of."

"I just thought she might be. She seems so busy with stuff outside of school lately."

"I think it's just that her mom's doing a big push for her career."

"Yeah."

Kristin finally realized what Josh was trying to get at. He was trying to find out if Monica had a boyfriend. It hadn't dawned on her that Josh was interested in Monica, but now that she thought about it, it made sense. Ever since the spring dance—when he and Monica had danced together—Josh had been asking about her, trying to find out when Monica would be around. Kristin wondered if her friend had picked up on his interest.

"Well, I guess I'd better get back to the world of

bank robberies and murder," he joked, changing the subject.

"So we're really going to do this party?"

"Absolutely. How about if I meet you outside here tomorrow after school and let you know then if we really can have it at my house?"

"Okay. Make sure Grady doesn't follow you."

"Yeah." Josh started up the stairs. "See you tomorrow."

"Okay."

" 'Bye."

Kristin started out across the lawn. She had to admit one thing about her new friends. They kept on surprising her.

3

"OH, YA, I VILL MAKE YOU SO BEAUTIFUL, DAWLING."

Nadia Lawrence leaned back in the padded leather chair at Stephanie of Sweden, the exclusive Beverly Hills facial salon. The most glamorous junior at Sunset High School was almost unrecognizable. Her long, reddish hair was pulled back, and her perfect body was concealed under a white cotton sheet. Nadia tried to smile, but her mouth was immobile, stuck shut by the thick layer of drying green mud that was tightening over her beautiful face.

"You have lovely skin. But too much sun." Eva, the Swedish facial consultant, clucked disapprovingly. "You California girls vill never listen to me."

Nadia squirmed under the sheet. She'd worked hard getting her tan just the right shade, and she didn't want anybody, *anybody,* messing with it. Still, she hadn't much choice now. Glennie Taryton, the richest junior at Sunset High, had asked her to accompany her for her biweekly facial, and Nadia, of course, had decided to come along.

"You tell her, Eva," teased Glennie, who lay on the chair next to Nadia. Glennie's skin was perfect porcelain white. She smiled at Nadia and pushed back her straight ash blond hair.

Nadia couldn't help wondering why Glennie had extended the invitation. The Rodeo Drive facial salon was a big deal—things were so exclusive at Stephanie of Sweden that even the cold cream was supposed to be kept in a safe. But what made Glennie's invitation so strange was that lately the rich girl had been giving Nadia a difficult time. Glennie had barely spoken to her during the last few weeks. Nadia recalled that she hadn't even been able to get Glennie to notice when she wore a brand new Yves St. Laurent creation that had the other girls at Sunset drooling with envy.

There was no doubt about it; Glennie's iciness had been driving Nadia crazy. But this sudden warmth made Nadia even more uneasy. What could Glennie have in mind? Nadia eyed the classic-featured beauty as she stretched out her long, willowy limbs in the chair next to Nadia's. Eva had just begun applying the green muck to Glennie's face.

"Nadia . . ."

"Yes, Glennie."

"Didn't I tell you you'd love this?" Glennie asked. "Jaclyn Smith comes here all the time."

"Mmm," Nadia managed.

"This mud is from the Dead Sea. It does *divine* things to your skin." Glennie's voice was so musical that she practically sang. She reached over and touched Nadia's hand. "You know, Nadia, it's a good thing you could come today. I've been wanting ..."

"Don't speak too much," Eva scolded. "Vonce you start to dry, don't move your face. You don't vant to crack de mask." She finished slathering Glennie. Before leaving, she dimmed the lights in the room and flicked a wall switch, causing both girls' chairs to vibrate softly.

Nadia looked up at the pale pink ceiling. The mud began to tighten around her nose.

"Nadia."

"Yes, Glennie," Nadia replied, trying to move her mouth as little as possible.

Glennie glanced over. "Nadia, you know, there's been a lot of talk about you lately."

Nadia tensed. She had been trying to ignore the looks she was getting, the whispers that passed when she walked down a Sunset corridor. She lay there paralyzed, waiting to hear what Glennie had to say.

Glennie reached up and patted her face with her fingertip. Deciding that the clay was still wet enough for further conversation, she took a deep breath. "Nadia, I just thought you should know that some people have been saying that the whole romance between you and Scott Sawyer was a fake."

"What!!!" Nadia gasped, sitting up with a violent start. She grimaced wildly and felt the dry clay crack into a hundred tiny lines. Desperate, she looked over at Glennie.

The rich girl just put a finger to her lips and uttered a little cry. "Oh, Nadia, you cracked. Now, don't you dare talk to me until I'm dry." With that, Glennie pulled up her sheet, breathed a satisfied sigh, and closed her eyes.

Nadia desperately tried to hold on to her emotions. She couldn't afford a real outburst in front of supercontrolled Glennie. She was being tested, and the slightest speck of insecurity would seal her fate. If she failed, she'd be cast off by Glennie and everyone else who mattered and thrown onto the trash heap along with a dozen other girls at Sunset who used to be popular. But this news ... it was awful. In the last few weeks Nadia had suspected her popularity was slipping and it terrified her; terrified her so much that she refused to face the real cause. But there was no denying it now. She had been found out, and Glennie was telling her to her face. People knew about Scott Sawyer.

Just thinking about the sexy, hot young movie actor made Nadia's head pound. She wished she'd never fabricated a romance with him. At least she should have had the good sense not to tell her classmates that he was going to be her date at the Sunset spring dance. Unfortunately Scott hadn't cooperated, but Nadia had assumed she'd pulled it off anyway by spreading the news that her producer father couldn't spare Scott from the set where they were shooting that night. To think that everyone had known the love affair was a sham made her ache with humiliation.

Suddenly the chair stopped vibrating, and Nadia jumped slightly as she felt a damp cloth pressing against her cheek. It was only Eva standing over her, smiling, gently wiping the dried mud from her face.

"Oh, look how beautiful you are now," the woman purred.

Nadia waited breathlessly for Glennie to be swabbed down too. Then she tried to laugh carelessly, but her chuckle came out in short uneven stabs. "That whole thing with Scott Sawyer was pretty funny, wasn't it," she said quickly.

Glennie waited for Eva to finish, then she sat up, her skin glowing a healthy pink, her white blond hair falling in a perfect line to her shoulders.

"Nadia, I wouldn't joke about it if I were you," she threatened. Her voice was no longer musical, and it made Nadia shiver. "I asked you to come here today because I wanted to tell you that if you don't do something major soon to put yourself back on the map, you are going to be dead socially. I've seen it happen before, and I just wanted to warn you."

Nadia felt as if the breath had been sucked out of her body. The walls of the little room seemed to close in on her. "Thanks for telling me," she croaked.

Having dropped the bomb, Glennie got up and slipped on her starched yellow shirt. Turning back, she gave Nadia a cool smile. "What are friends for?"

"Yes." Nadia sat up on the padded lounge chair. She tried to think. She had to do something to put herself back on top. Nadia couldn't believe she'd let things go this far. But she was so shocked, so panicked, that she couldn't force her usually crafty mind to function coherently.

"There's a screening of the new Steven Spielberg movie next week at one of the studios," she said, grasping at straws. "My dad has tickets. Maybe I should take Mindy and Lisa and Marilyn and everybody," Nadia suggested, referring to their crowd of wealthy, good-looking girls.

Glennie barely reacted. Instantly Nadia knew it was a rotten idea. A studio movie screening was not that big a deal. Glennie's boyfriend worked for Universal; they probably went to screenings all the time. Nadia had to think of something very special that only she could offer.

Eva popped her head back in to hand Glennie a tiny jar of the special Stephanie of Sweden skin cream. It must have cost a hundred dollars an ounce. As Eva started to back out, Glennie stopped her.

"Eva, is Linda Evans coming in today?" Glennie's lyrical voice was edged with excitement. It wasn't often that cool, calculating Glennie got excited.

Eva shook her head. "Oh, no. She hasn't been in since last month." Eva smiled at Nadia. "She is so beautiful, that Miss Evans. Beautiful skin." Quietly Eva waved good-bye and pulled the door shut behind her.

That was it! Of course! Nadia had a brilliant idea. Why hadn't she thought of it before?

The one thing she could offer ... the thing that made even Glennie lose her cool ... was movie stars. When Glennie ran into someone famous—like the actors and actresses who had been dinner guests of Nadia's parents for as long as she could remember—Glennie went crazy with excitement. And she wasn't the only one. Other kids at school went just as nutty. Sure, lots of their parents were in the entertainment business, but few were as powerful or well connected as Nadia's producer father. Nadia wondered if one reason for the Scott Sawyer backlash against her was simply because her friends had never been given a chance to meet the actor. But now, if she could give them something even *better* than Scott Sawyer ...

Nadia hopped down off the chair, her reddish hair spilling over her shoulders as she pulled on her Guess jeans. The energy returned to her lithe body as hope surged through her again. *Her father's party!* That was it. Her producer father was throwing a big bash for all the bigwigs in Hollywood, and when George Lawrence called, everybody came running. She glanced over at Glennie, who was pulling on her Ralph Lauren slacks.

"Glennie, I was thinking. . . . My father is having this big Hollywood party the weekend after next." Nadia smiled as she saw that Glennie's gray eyes were now all attention. "Do you think I should try to invite some kids at school? Tons of stars will be there."

Glennie's mouth fell open and she rushed over. "Oh, Nadia, that would be just the thing."

"Do you think so?"

Glennie slid up on the chair next to Nadia and touched her hand. "Oh, yes! But only if you handle it just right." Glennie tapped her playfully on the wrist with her comb, and Nadia knew that she was on the way back up. "Let me tell you how to do it."

"Yes, Glennie."

"First, you have to make it very exclusive. Let everyone know about it, but only invite about ten kids. They should be from different crowds, too. All the best people of course, but just one or so from each group. That way it will be real status to be asked, and then each person will go back to his or her crowd praising you. Do you understand?"

"Yes, Glennie."

"Now, Nadia, you have to invite the right people. Call me and I'll help you make a list."

Nadia slid down off the chair, and the girls walked out into the front reception area, where they waited to pay their bill. "Of course, you and David are the first people I'm inviting," Nadia cooed.

Glennie cocked her head to one side and smiled. "Really? Us? Oh, Nadia, you are so sweet. I'll let you know if we can come."

Nadia was more than a little irritated by the last remark. How typical of Glennie to set her up for a big party and then act as if her and David's coming would be doing Nadia a big favor. But Nadia held her tongue and blithely examined her nails. There were bigger stakes here, and both of them knew it.

Glennie picked up her tab and looked it over, then she managed that cool, pristine "Glennie" smile.

"Now, you make sure to check with me on all the details. As long as you can get the right people to come, this will be just the thing to make everybody forget about the spring dance."

"Glennie, I don't know what I'd do without you."

"Oh, Nadia, you know how I am. I just like helping people."

"I know." Nadia took out her Gucci wallet and started to pay for her beauty treatment. Glennie stopped her.

"Just put us both on my charge," Glennie told the woman behind the antique desk. Glennie turned back to Nadia. "My treat. After all, I asked you to come with me."

"Thank you, Glennie."

Nadia smiled demurely and folded her arms across her silk knit sweater.

❀ 4

PLOP . . .

Monica stared as a huge raindrop struck the puddle forming in front of her. She tried to hold back a growing feeling of panic.

Monica had an audition this afternoon—for a part in a Jack Lemmon movie where she would play the role of his punk rock daughter. It was a small but memorable part, and Monica had thought it out carefully and had tried to dress exactly in character. This morning she had settled on a huge white tee-shirt, tight black pants, and high-top red tennies. Still, it hadn't been quite daring enough. Monica had mulled it over all day in school, then in the middle of sixth-period French class inspiration had hit. Between sixth and seventh periods she'd raced to the bathroom and drawn a chaotic design on the tee-shirt with two colored Magic Markers. It had looked perfect at the time, but there had been one fatal flaw: The Magic Markers weren't waterproof.

PLOP . . . PLOP . . . PLOP . . .

Monica looked at the steady rain and wanted to tear her hair. Why, oh, why, hadn't she picked up her Honda Accord from the shop where it was being fixed? They'd called and said her car was ready three days ago, but she just hadn't gotten around to it. The weather had been nice, and she'd preferred riding her Vespa motor scooter to school instead. If only she'd listened to the weather report today! If she went out in the rain, her shirt would turn into a mess, and she'd end up looking like a dripping piece of abstract art.

"Darn it, rain!"

Monica stamped her now squeaky tennis shoes and stared dejectedly at her motor scooter. Her head was starting to ache, and she felt like screaming. She couldn't mess up; this was too important. She looked down. Already the red and blue lines were beginning to bleed together. There was a splotch of dye on the side of her arm.

Next she noticed her damp notebook. "Oh, no," Monica moaned. One corner of her photo and resume was peeking out. It was wet and limp.

Monica squeezed her eyes shut for a second and tried to figure out what to do. She couldn't call her mother. Her mother would be furious and would only remind Monica that she'd given her daughter a car on her sixteenth birthday so they both could avoid last-minute emergencies like this. Monica checked her Mickey Mouse watch. The rain was getting heavier, now falling over the parking lot in a solid, steamy sheet. She checked her watch again. On the verge of tears, she prayed that she would somehow get to her audition on time.

"C'mon, rain," Monica stammered, "give me a break."

Just outside the white stucco building that housed the media room, Kristin Sullivan stood in the same pouring rain waiting for Josh. The water streamed down her face, dripping off her French braid and soaking her light cotton blouse. But it wasn't a cold Minnesota rain; it was tropical and pleasant. Even if it hadn't been so warm, however, she would have rushed outside to avoid being seen by Grady. She was determined to keep this party a secret; she wanted it to be a real surprise for Grady. Finally Josh appeared. He skulked by in a huge army-green rain tarp.

"Hey, Josh. Josh!" Kristin called. He didn't hear her. She wondered if he had his Walkman on under the plastic hood. Sure enough, he was tapping his thigh at weird rhythmic intervals. Obviously he was listening to his futuristic, new-age music again.

Kristin ran over and pulled on his arm. He flung around, surprised, and started to laugh.

"Hi," he said with a grin. He looked up at the rain happily, letting the water spill onto his face. "Great rain."

Kristin laughed. "Is Grady gone? Is it okay to go inside?" she asked.

Josh nodded. "Yeah, but not in here near the media room. Follow me."

Kristin followed Josh as they ran around the building until they reached the back door. As quickly as possible they slipped in, finding themselves just outside the attendance office. Both panting, they looked around and giggled.

"Safe at last," Kristin said, as she shook the water off the top of her notebook.

Josh pushed down the hood of his tarp and took off his earphones. "I wasn't sure where you went."

"I know. I started to walk right up to you and then I saw Grady. So I just waited outside. I just kept hoping you'd come out." Kristen caught a line of water that was running down her nose.

Josh laughed. "I couldn't get rid of him. He decided he wanted to talk after class. You know, one of those big conversations about *life* that he likes to get into—where we'll all be in the future, what's the meaning of reality—little things like that. I kept trying to think of a one-word answer. I think he finally gave up."

"You're sure he's gone?"

"Pretty sure."

They both paused to check and make sure that Grady was nowhere in sight. At the same time they turned back to each other and leaned in excitedly.

"Okay. What did you find out?"

"We're on," Josh beamed. "We can have the party at my house a week from this Saturday night."

Kristin jumped, her deck shoes oozing water when she came down. "That's perfect! I'll take care of all the food and everything, but you have to help me with the invitations. I still don't know all of Grady's friends."

Josh took off his steamed-up glasses and wiped them on the cuff of his rugby shirt.

"Sure. Let me give you my address and phone number, so you can pass it on." Kristin held out her math book as Josh pulled a felt-tip pen out of his notebook and wrote it down. The letters instantly bled on the damp brown-paper cover. "Tell everybody to be here right at eight. We'll figure out a way to keep Grady from showing up until eight-thirty or so."

"I'll have to think of a good excuse." Kristin grinned. She turned her book around and read the address. It was in Culver City, a much less wealthy community south of Beverly Hills. Kristin had thought kids had to live in Beverly Hills in order to go to Sunset, but obviously not. Josh drew her a crude map and scrawled in his phone number.

"Okay, so I'll start spreading the word," he said.

Kristin looked at the map and blew on the ink to dry it. "Just make sure everybody keeps it supersecret. It has to be a surprise. That's the main thing."

"Right."

They both started to walk toward the main entrance. When they were within a few feet of the door it swung open furiously. The small figure hurtled through so intently that it took Kristin a moment to realize that it was Monica.

"Monica!" Josh said. "Are you okay?"

Monica looked up. "Kristin!" she said, ignoring Josh and rushing over to her good friend. Just seeing Kristin's calm, open face made her feel a little better. "I have this audition in Hollywood in half an hour and I rode my scooter today. I was just going to call my mom and ask her what to do."

"I can drive you ..." Kristin started to say, but Josh interrupted her.

"I drove today. I can take you there," he volunteered hopefully.

Monica seemed to hear only Kristin. "K, can you really take me? Oh, that would be great."

"No problem."

Josh cleared his throat. "If you can't drive her, I can," he said casually to Kristin. Kristin waited to see if Monica would pick up his hint.

"That's okay, Josh," Monica said, giving Kristin's arm an affectionate pat. "You are a true friend, K. Thanks. I'm due there really soon, so if we could get going ..."

The girls walked back outside. Josh followed patiently. The rain had turned to a light drizzle, but the sky was still ominously gray. Monica's short, layered hair was forming wispy ringlets from the humidity.

"It's a good thing you found us," Kristin said as they cut across the parking lot.

Monica was walking ahead of her, moving so fast she was almost running. "I know. And I painted on this tee-shirt with Magic Marker. You know, sort of a costume ..."

"Costume?" Kristin asked.

Monica shrugged. "Yeah, I'm auditioning for the part of somebody's punked-out daughter. What do you think?"

Kristin and Joshua both laughed. They reached Kristin's mom's rusty old station wagon, and Kristin and Monica climbed in. Josh leaned back against the car in the next space and gazed at Monica. He hadn't taken his eyes off her, but Monica, who was riffling through her notebook, seemed too preoccupied to notice.

"Have a good audition," he said, leaning on Monica's open window.

Monica looked up from her notebook for just a moment. "Thanks, Josh." She smiled. Her eyes didn't linger. She went right back to her notes.

Josh hesitated, but when he did not get any more response from Monica he began to walk away. The rain broke again, and he quickened to a graceful run.

" 'Bye, Josh," Kristin called, starting the ignition.

Monica pulled up her legs Indian-style and laid her notebook across her lap. "Thanks, Kristin. This is great of you to do this. You can just drop me off and I'll call my mom to come get me." Monica pulled down the visor and examined her face. Her eye makeup was only slightly smeared. She corrected it with a wet finger.

Kristin maneuvered the bulky car out of the parking lot. "I'm not in a hurry. I'll wait for you if you want."

"Honest? You can come in and just sit in the waiting room. It's not all that interesting, but it might be fun."

Kristin pulled into the busy Beverly Hills traffic and looked over excitedly. "You mean I could actually sit in the room and wait while you're auditioning? I'd love to! I can write about this in my next ten letters to Amy."

Monica giggled and nervously checked her painted shirt. She was very keyed up. "We have to go to Melrose near Highland, but it's okay. You don't have to get on the freeway."

Kristin was relieved. She was slowly getting used to the busy surface driving in L.A., but changing lanes on the freeway still gave her the jitters. She always made Monica turn around and give her the go-ahead before she switched lanes.

Chewing on her thumbnail, Monica rolled up her window. The rain was getting heavy again. "I just kept thinking of showing up for this audition dripping wet. I could just hear my mom's voice when I called her afterward and told her I didn't get it because I went in looking like a drowned rat." Monica looked anxiously in the mirror again. "I hope I'm not late." She gave a quick look behind her as they neared Wilshire Boulevard. "You can go, K. You're clear."

Kristin surged ahead and joined the heavy afternoon traffic. "Is this for that Tom Selleck movie?"

Monica sighed in frustration. "That was yesterday. Anyway, forget the Tom Selleck movie. They said I was too old."

"Too old? How old was the part supposed to be?"

"Sixteen. I guess I was one month too old. If I'd auditioned last month, I'm sure they would have told me I was too young." They both laughed.

"So what are you auditioning for today?"

"A movie starring Jack Lemmon. It's a small

part—his daughter—and she appears in just one scene."

"Maybe you should have shown up soaking wet—you might have looked more punk."

"Yeah, with my luck, then they'd tell me I was too punk."

Kristin gave her a supportive smile. "I bet you get this one. I don't know why. I just have a feeling."

"I hope you're right," Monica replied wistfully. "I could sure use a yes for a change." She stared out the window as they passed the hip clothing and antique stores of Melrose Avenue. "What were you doing after school? Is there anything new going on with the media class?"

Kristin shook her head. "I stayed to talk to Josh. Oh, I didn't tell you yet—we're throwing a big surprise party for Grady's eighteenth birthday. He's been so bummed about Yale, we want to give him a big bash to cheer him up."

"That'll be great!" Monica replied, thinking how great it was of Kristin to plan such a party. Of course, she wasn't surprised, remembering how, right from the start, she'd been drawn to Kristin's gentleness and generosity. It was funny, but whenever she was with Kristin or Grady and his friends like Josh and Eddie, the pressures of her life seemed to fade.

"Do you want me to help?" Monica volunteered. "I could maybe make decorations, or help with the food or something."

"Eddie's doing the decorations, but if you could help me with the food, that would be great. I think there's going to be a lot of people. It's a week from this Saturday night at Josh's house."

"A week from Saturday?" Monica repeated. The calmness disappeared and the familiar tug-o'-war started again. Hoping against hope, she quickly leafed through her diary. But no, Grady's bash *was* the same night as the Lawrences' party. Monica knew she would have to make a decision. "Kristin ..." she began tentatively.

"Hmm?" Kristin squinted, trying to see the street numbers as they drove down Melrose. She spotted the address of Monica's audition and turned onto a residential sidestreet to park.

Monica hesitated until after Kristin had turned off the engine. "Kristin, I don't think I can go to Grady's party."

Kristin turned to her. "Why not?"

"I have to go to this big affair at the Lawrences' with my mom. It's for Nadia's parents, not Nadia," Monica said quickly, not meeting Kristin's eyes. She knew what her friend's reaction would be when she mentioned Nadia. It was because of Nadia that Kristin's move to Beverly Hills had been so difficult. Monica didn't like their haughty classmate any more than Kristin did, but she knew what she had to do. "There are going to be people there I have to meet. It's important for my career."

Kristin leaned on the steering wheel. She looked very surprised ... and hurt. There was a long pause. "Do you want to go to this party at the Lawrences'?"

Monica rubbed her forehead as if she could get

rid of the tightness inside. "That doesn't have anything to do with it. If I'm going to get ahead as an actress, I have to start doing things like that— meeting people, being in the right places, using the people that I know...."

Kristin pulled the keys out and jangled them against her palm. Her green eyes were filled with disappointment. "This party for Grady is important too. You're the closest friend I have here."

"I know. I don't want to let you down, but there are just some things I have to do," Monica repeated dully. Her voice sounded emotionless. "It's for that TV series I told you about. It might all hinge on my being seen at that party. Otherwise I would never miss something for Grady. You know how it is."

"I guess."

The two girls looked at each other for a moment.

"I'm not the only one who's going to miss you," Kristin said in a funny voice.

"What do you mean?" Monica pulled her picture and resume out of her notebook. She didn't want to talk about this anymore.

Kristin didn't move. "I think Josh was hoping the party might be a chance for you two to get together."

"What?"

"Come on, you must have noticed that Josh likes you. I think he's pretty cute myself."

"Josh Ross?"

Kristin laughed. "What other Josh do you know? I can't believe you haven't noticed."

Monica scratched her head, her dark bangs

falling into her eyes. "I haven't noticed anything. All I've been thinking about are these auditions and that series I'm up for. I've never really thought about him, not much anyway. Are you sure he really likes me?"

"Positive."

Monica made herself think back to her mother's advice. "You're sure?"

Kristin shrugged. "He's never come out and told me point blank, but as much as it's possible to figure out those kinds of things, yeah, I'm sure."

Monica sat up. "That's perfect," she said. "I bet he wouldn't mind helping me, then."

"What are you talking about?"

"You know my advanced biology class?"

Kristin nodded. She knew that Monica was in trouble in the class and worried that a bad grade might affect her ability to accept acting work.

"Josh is in my class and he's an incredible brain. I've been having some trouble in the course and so I offered to do a special make-up paper. Well, you know how hard Mr. Groener is—and I'm hopeless in science—but if Josh helped me ..." Monica laid her notebook on the floor and, holding on to her photo and resume, opened the car door.

Kristin stopped her, her face serious. "Monica, you wouldn't take advantage of him to help you just because he likes you."

"Of course not," Monica reacted, but something caught in her voice. She was starting to feel as if there were two different Monicas inside her, fighting it out, tugging at both ends. She tried to think what her mother would say. If Josh didn't want to help her, he was welcome to say no. She had to take advantage of every opportunity. She had to use the people she knew to help her get ahead. This situation with Josh was a perfect example.

"Just don't lead him on," Kristin warned.

Monica nodded. She didn't want to lead anybody on. She just wanted to have a career. Kristin was refreshingly honest and straightforward; still, she had no idea how Hollywood operated. Even when she was little, Monica had seen the way it worked. The actress who played the oldest sister on "The Twain Family" had flirted with and manipulated everybody on the set—the director, the elderly propman, even her fellow actors. And she had gotten everything she'd wanted, from the best dressing room to the most close-ups. Now the actress was an up-and-coming movie star.

"Don't worry," Monica told Kristin.

"I just wouldn't want to see Josh get hurt."

Monica avoided Kristin's gaze and got out of the car. "Let's go in. It's time."

"Okay. Oh ... good luck."

Monica gave her a tight smile as they hurried over to Melrose Avenue.

❀ 5

THE LOW, SPANISH-STYLE BUNGALOW HAD A SMALL WAITING room. The furniture didn't match, and the room smelled of stale cigarette smoke, but there was an air of glamour and excitement nonetheless. Partly it was the framed posters that lined the walls— posters advertising the famous movies that had previously been cast by June Webster's casting office. But mostly the electricity came from the six or seven teenagers who were waiting to audition.

They were examining their photos and resumes, redoing their hair, or nervously pacing across the well-worn carpet. All were attractive and had an aura of being someone very special. Kristin immediately recognized a beautiful blonde as the actress she had seen only a week before as George Segal's daughter in a television movie. Next to her was a serious-looking girl who faced the corner gesturing to the wall and practicing lines in a whispery voice. Another actress sat on the sofa, fixing her makeup with the concentration of a great painter.

Monica walked right past them. She headed for the reception desk and checked in with a young male secretary. He took her picture and resume and handed her a few typed pages of dialogue.

"Thank you," Monica said. She quickly came back and sat down next to Kristin.

"Even I'm nervous now," Kristin whispered. "This is as bad as going to the dentist."

Monica nodded anxiously. The next moment a door on the other side of the room opened and a tall, good-looking young woman appeared. The woman was obviously in charge. Everyone perked up when she came in.

"Who's that?" Kristin whispered.

"I'm pretty sure it's June Webster, the casting director," Monica whispered back, never taking her eyes off Ms. Webster.

"What does she do?"

Monica sat on the edge of the old leather couch. "She organizes the audition, decides what actors to bring in. Then the director or producer picks who they want to hire. But she's usually the one who tells you if you got it or not."

June quickly looked over the room for her next auditioner. She gestured to the blonde from the television movie. The actress immediately stood up, gave a big forced smile, and followed June into an inner office. Just before the door closed again, a handsome, well-built guy came out and left quickly by the front door.

"I'm going to look over the script," Monica explained to Kristin, referring to her typed pages. Monica then leaned forward and read the pages over and over, devouring every word. She mouthed the lines to herself, trying different readings. Soon she was totally enmeshed in the scene. She forgot about Kristin, the other actors, her problem with Grady's party. It was a funny scene between a father and daughter, and the more Monica read it over, the more confident she became. She had the rare feeling she knew just what they wanted.

Kristin watched with fascination. She had never seen Monica at work before, and she was amazed at the concentration in her friend's face. She was also stunned by the intensity of Monica's desire, the hope that this audition be *the* one. Kristin could see it in everyone—not just Monica. Two actresses who sat on the floor across from her were discussing a previous audition, trying to figure out why a certain actress had been selected rather than either of them. They thought of every excuse—the girl who had been hired had known someone; they had been too tall for the leading man; the director was in a bad mood when they had auditioned; it was their agent's fault. This audition was going to be different, they told each other. They both could just feel it.

"Monica Miller," announced a low, professional voice. June Webster stood in the doorway once more. The casting director slipped on a pair of practical, mannish glasses and looked over Monica's photo and resume.

"Good luck," Kristin whispered as her friend looked up.

Monica gave her a frantic smile. Clearing her throat, Monica followed June into the inner office.

Just as she went through the doorway, she turned back to give her friend one last nervous grimace. Kristin held up her crossed fingers.

Kristin sat for a few moments, listening to snatches of show-biz gossip. By this time her heart was pounding, and she had butterflies of her own. She felt almost as if she were auditioning too. When someone touched her gently on the knee she reacted with a jumpy start.

"Hi," said an amused male voice.

Kristin shifted on the sofa and looked over. When she saw the face of the boy seated beside her, she almost gasped out loud. He was one of the handsomest guys she'd ever seen.

He had straight black hair that was very short except for a few curly wisps that he had purposefully let grow long at the back of his neck. His eyes were large, cobalt blue, and rimmed by thick dark lashes. His nose was straight and long, he had cheekbones that would have made any model envious, and he smelled of aftershave. He wore an exquisite blue suit and shiny black loafers. Kristin even noticed he was wearing a pair of dark socks with clocks woven into the pattern.

"They're a little weird, aren't they?" He pulled up his pant legs slightly.

Kristin looked up startled. "What ..."

"My socks, but don't worry. Everybody notices them. They're from this great antique clothing store down on Melrose."

Kristin giggled and the boy's eyes sparkled. Kristin thought they were the most beautiful eyes she had ever seen and so electric ... it was like accidentally sticking a knife in a toaster. Kristin almost felt like fanning herself, but was too embarrassed. She also realized that if it weren't for Grady, she'd probably fall instantly in love.

"Did they give you a script to look at?" he asked casually, seemingly oblivious to her gaping.

"I'm just waiting for my friend. I'm not auditioning," Kristin answered, recovering her composure.

The actor laced his hands together and leaned forward on his elbows. Kristin noticed he was wearing gold cufflinks. "They said just a few of the girls are reading. I guess the guys are here for extra parts. That's good that your friend got to read. She must have a good agent."

"Her agent better be good," Kristin laughed. "It's her own mother."

"Oh, yeah?" He smiled. His teeth were straight and very white. "What's her name?"

"Monica Miller. Her mom's name is Rosalind Miller."

"Sure, Rosalind Miller. She's really big, but I've been meeting tons of agents. I can't remember if I met her or not. They all tell you how good they are and how much they're going to help you. It's really hard to decide what agent to go with."

Kristin was fascinated. She had always thought that it was hard for young actors to get an agent to represent them. But she could understand that this actor, with his looks and self-assurance, would have agents fighting over him.

"Well, wish me luck," the actor said warmly.

Then he turned away from Kristin and started talking to another girl across the room.

Down in the hall, inside Ms. Webster's office, Monica could tell that her reading was going very well. Her mind was clear, her body energized, and she was not the least bit self-conscious. If anything, her confusion about Grady's party had only made her more keyed-up and emotional. And that seemed to be what they were looking for. Monica had even understood what was funny in the scene and why. She had actually made the director laugh out loud.

The director grinned. "Okay, Monica, thank you."

Monica smiled back. She hesitated before exiting. After a good audition, Monica always wanted to stay longer. She never wanted to give back the script or leave until they assured her she had the part—which, of course, they never did. But she was a professional, so she thanked June and Stephen Book, the bearded director, and got up to go.

Just as she reached the door to the outer office, June stopped her.

"That was a wonderful reading, Monica," June said in her clear, authoritative voice.

Monica felt a swell of pride and tugged on her huge white tee-shirt. "Thank you."

June smiled. "Can you get out of school next Friday to shoot?"

Monica told herself not to get her hopes up. June had not said yes yet. Still, her body was starting to feel like a highflying kite. "Yes."

June leaned in and spoke softly. "Don't say anything to the other girls waiting to read, but Stephen has decided he wants you to do the part."

"Really?" It took Monica a moment to believe she had heard right. She took in a huge gulp of air and grinned.

June laughed. "Really. Tell your mother I'll be calling her."

It was beginning to sink in, and Monica had to control herself. She wanted to jump up and down, grab June Webster around the neck and holler. "Oh, thank you," Monica bubbled as June led her back out into the waiting room. "That's great. That's wonderful. Oh—thanks."

When Monica reappeared in the waiting room, all her uneasiness was gone. Her high-topped tennis shoes felt like those crazy boots with springs on the bottom, the ones from the cartoons. It was only a small part—just one day's work—but it was in the new Jack Lemmon movie, and best of all, they had liked her; they had said yes!!! She plopped down next to Kristin and bounced on the sofa like a three-year-old.

"How did it go?" Kristin asked eagerly.

"Great." Monica gave Kristin's arm an affectionate squeeze, then leaned over and whispered in her ear. "I got it!!!" She quickly gestured for secrecy with a finger up to her lips. Kristin gave her a big hug.

Monica started to bound up again when she turned and found herself face to face with the boy in the suit. The actor extended his hand, but

Monica forgot to take it. As she looked into the young man's dazzling dark eyes, she almost felt faint. She'd never met a boy before who had actually made her feel woozy. When she didn't accept his offer of a handshake, he reached up, gently took Monica's hand away from her face, and wrapped her small palm in his.

"Hi. I'm Warren Taylor. I was talking to your friend."

"Hi." Monica stared at him. "Oh, I'm Monica Miller."

"Your audition went well?" Warren's eyes never left hers.

"Uh-huh," Monica breathed.

"I bet you wowed them," he said slowly, with an approving nod.

"What makes you say that?"

"Oh, I can always spot talent a mile away."

There was a lull in the conversation as Warren and Monica gazed at each other. Kristin couldn't help thinking that if there had been a chance for Josh before, there certainly wasn't one now. Sitting between Warren and Monica made her feel as if she were in the middle of an electrical field. It was a little embarrassing. Kristin got up and moved to the other side of the room.

Just then she realized that June Webster was standing right next to her, bending over the desk, checking the list of actors to be auditioned. The next moment, the casting director was looking directly at her. June slipped off her glasses, her lightly made-up eyes going over Kristin's face like a well-trained camera.

"Who are you?" June asked. She stepped back to get a better look at Kristin and chewed on the stem of her glasses.

Kristin looked behind her to make sure that the woman was really talking to her. "I'm Kristin Sullivan."

"How old are you?" June fired off.

"Sixteen. Almost seventeen."

June seemed amused by the answer. "Have you done anything?"

Kristin wasn't sure what to say, but something about June's curious, warm expression helped her along. "I danced in a rock video at Sunset High and in a dance concert at my old school in Minnesota."

June nodded and looked down at her list again. Suddenly she put her arm around Kristin. "Would you like to come back and meet the director?"

Kristin stood there for a moment in delirious shock. Of course she'd love to, although she was scared and nervous that she wouldn't know what to do or say when she got there. She looked over at Monica, but her friend was so involved in talking to Warren that Kristin couldn't get her attention. Her heart pounding, Kristin nodded and followed June back to the inner office.

She walked down a short, carpeted hall and into an elegant office done all in beige and peach tones. The room was dominated by a large desk, the top of which was covered with lists, photos of actors, a telephone, scripts, and half-full mugs of coffee. June slipped in behind her desk and gestured for Kristin to sit in a canvas director's chair in the middle of the room.

"Hello, Kristin Sullivan," said a bearded man in what Kristin guessed was his mid-thirties. He was slumped down in a chair next to June and wore a beat-up jean jacket over a Rolling Stones tee-shirt. He was smiling.

"This is Stephen Book, the director," announced June. She went to take a sip of her coffee and made a terrible face. She glared at Stephen Book as if he were a naughty child.

"Stephen," she laughed, "what did you put in here?"

He grinned sheepishly and held up a bottle of something green and awful-looking. "Plant protein. It's good for you. It will help you relax."

June gave him a frustrated smile. "You are hopeless," she said, slipping on her glasses and returning to business. "Kristin is a dancer," she told him in a no-nonsense voice. "She has a fresh, Midwest look. I thought she might be a good addition to the party scene."

Stephen stood up and stared down at Kristin. Blatantly he looked her up and down as if, Kristin thought, she were something on sale at a department store. Hands on his hips, he walked up to her.

"Wanna dance?" he asked cheekishly.

Kristin had a moment of total confusion. She looked at June and then back to the bearded director, who was expectantly holding out his hand to her. Was he teasing her or just fooling around? She didn't know, but responding to the silly look on his face, Kristin stood up impulsively and took his hand. He took off in a wild jitterbug.

Kristin began to giggle and dance too. She was just beginning to think she was making a total fool out of herself when the director stopped dancing, patted her on the shoulder, and said, "You're hired."

Kristin froze. She couldn't believe it! Obviously the spontaneous dance was Stephen Book's form of an audition. She looked at June, who was shaking her head as if she were indulging a spoiled child. Kristin collapsed into her chair, her legs buckling beneath her.

"Kristin, can you get out of school next Friday to shoot?" the casting director asked.

Kristin's eyes opened wide. She wasn't sure how it had happened, but she really was being offered a job in a Hollywood movie. "I think so!"

"We'll need you for one day," June explained as she wrote something on one of her stacks of paper. "No lines, just dancing in the background. The pay is forty dollars. You won't have to join the union." She handed Kristin a card to write down her phone number and address. "I'll call you and let you know the time and what to wear." June stood up and walked to the door.

Kristin just stared at her. She was still in shock over her incredible stroke of luck. Her friends back in Minnesota would go crazy when they heard about this! Suddenly she realized that June's moving to the door was to let Kristin know that it was time for her to leave.

"Thanks," she said to Stephen Book as she stood up. He was now riffling through the photos and resumes. He lifted a preoccupied pinky to her in response.

When Kristin walked back into the waiting room she no longer looked at the lounging actors as a different breed—she would be one of them, for a single day at least. She rushed over to Monica, who was still sitting very close to Warren with an infatuated expression on her delicate face. As Kristin approached them she saw Monica give the handsome actor her phone number. In the same instant, June called Warren's name, and he lifted his head quickly and stood up.

"Think lucky thoughts for me," he whispered to Monica, caressing her arm. "I'll call you." He gave her a last, stunning smile and followed June into the inner office.

Kristin and Monica, both bursting with good fortune, rushed out of the waiting room and back outside. The rain had stopped completely; in fact, it had even washed away the smog, so that it was now a perfect spring afternoon.

"WAAAAHOOOOOO!" Monica yelled joyously as she bolted down the street toward the car. When she reached it she fell back against the side in a mock faint. "I am in love," she sighed, her hand to her heart. She began to laugh with a free, silvery giggle.

Kristin ran up beside her and slapped the side of the old station wagon. "Well, don't think you're the *only one* who gets to do anything exciting," she tantalized. "I'm going to be in the movie next Friday too, dancing in the background!"

Monica threw her arms around her friend. "You are!!! I hoped that was what had happened! Kristin, this is so great!"

Both girls laughed and whooped until they noticed a crabby old woman watering her lawn and giving them a disapproving stare. Giggling, they slid into the front seat. Having completely forgotten all her self-doubt, Monica was bubbling over like a bottle of champagne.

"What a great day," she marveled as Kristin pulled the old car away from the curb. "I got a speaking part; you are going to be in the movie too ..."

"And ..." Kristin teased.

Monica let out a delirious holler. "And I just gave my phone number to the most gorgeous guy in the entire world!!!"

The girls looked at each other, each sharing the other's victory and happiness. Monica stuck her head out the window as they sped along with the early evening traffic. Feeling the cool air against her face, she looked out at the clear California sky and felt that this was one of those rare moments in life that made it all worthwhile.

6

THE NEXT DAY AFTER SCHOOL NADIA LAWRENCE AND JT
Gantner lay on their backs doing buttock tucks at
Jane Fonda's Workout. It was almost the end of
the exercise class, and gorgeous, fit Nadia was
still going strong. But JT, who had always been
on the chubby side, lay on her gray mat, staring
blearily up at the ceiling. She thought she was
going to die.

"Go for the burn!" screamed the instructor, a
stunning black woman in a red leotard and leg
warmers. Her bare legs were flawlessly shaped.
She turned up the Bruce Springsteen song and
yelled even louder. "You put it there, you get rid
of it!"

JT groaned. She watched Nadia on the mat in
front of her. Her friend's figure was as perfect as
the instructor's. JT looked down at her own roundish thighs encased in a soaking pair of nylon
dance pants and felt like crying. She could go to
Jane Fonda's Workout every day for the next year,
and she'd never be gorgeous and lean like Nadia.

She blew her short blond hair away from her forehead and wiped her dewy, round cheeks with a small towel.

Nadia looked back at her. "Come on, JT. You can do it," she encouraged.

Nadia continued doing her tucks with fierce determination. That was one quality no one could accuse Nadia of lacking—determination. JT, who was not as determined, nodded weakly and joined in the last few times, lifting her hips into the air with a painful squeeze.

"That's it for today. Give yourselves a hand," the instructor announced at last. Everyone collapsed, applauded halfheartedly, and dragged their mats to the front of the large rectangular room. The mirrored studio was as damp as a rain forest. As the teacher opened the glass door, the mirrors began to uncloud.

Nadia picked up her Gucci purse and paused to examine herself in the mirror. Her lush, reddish hair was tied up in a thick ponytail, but sweaty wisps were curling all around her beautiful face. She patted her tanned skin with a tissue, being careful not to smear the dark pencil that lined her dramatic brown eyes. Turning to the side, she made sure that her stomach was perfectly flat. It was. No matter what people were saying about her at school, she knew she still looked terrific.

"JT, you're doing great," Nadia said sunnily as her friend slowly dragged herself up off the floor. "I can really see a difference."

JT looked in the mirror and frowned. Her face was sweet, almost babyish, and a single long earring hung down her neck. Her pale clear skin had turned very red from the exertion. She pulled a Camp Beverly Hills tee-shirt over her full bust and tried to smile.

"I'll get you a Perrier," Nadia said, hoping it would bring JT back to life. She slung her jeans over her shoulder and went out to the front desk.

JT leaned on the ballet barre to catch her breath. It was unusual for Nadia to be so thoughtful as to rush out and get her a bottle of water. The last few weeks Nadia had been making a considerable effort to be nice and considerate.

JT had always been loyal to Nadia, but recently she had been pushed to the limit. What had happened during the taping of the media class rock videos a few weeks before had been almost too much, even for JT. She had seen a cruel, ruthless side to Nadia that made her consider breaking away from her best friend. But since that time, Nadia had been going out of her way to be thoughtful and supportive, so JT had finally decided to forgive her. After all, Nadia had problems too. In fact, she'd been under a lot of strain recently, considering all the rumors that were circulating about how she had fabricated the whole romance between Scott Sawyer and herself.

JT made her way through the crowded foyer until she joined Nadia on the brick patio outside. Nadia was eating a frozen fruit bar and held up the Perrier bottle for JT.

"Thanks," JT said, gulping down the fizzy water. Her throat was parched, and she was still terribly overheated.

Nadia continued to encourage her. "Can you tell how much slimmer your hips are since you've been coming? I sure can," she said, stretching her back easily.

JT shrugged. "I guess." She wasn't fat like she used to be; still, her figure was so womanly and roundish that she always felt as if she were still too big everywhere.

Nadia smiled and patted her affectionately. "Let's walk up Beverly and look in the windows. I saw a jumpsuit up the street that is perfect for you."

"Okay." JT finished her Perrier and, gathering up her things, followed Nadia out onto the sidewalk.

It was a warm and hazy afternoon, and the traffic buzzed by, leaving a layer of exhaust behind. A few drivers slowed to gawk at Nadia— who was still in her designer exercise wear with her jeans slung over her shoulder. JT hoped that Nadia's beauty wouldn't cause a crack-up. They passed a couple of dancewear shops and a photo studio before stopping in front of a small boutique called Avanti Two.

"That's it," Nadia said sweetly, pointing to a dressy white jumpsuit with a wide leather belt. "In the middle of class I thought about that jumpsuit and how perfect it would be on you. It's a great special-occasion jumpsuit."

JT pulled on her earring and looked over at Nadia. The jumpsuit was nice, although it was a lot like the other outfits that Nadia had encouraged her to buy over the months they had been pals. Still, JT was flattered that Nadia was giving her so much thought. "Well, there's nothing too special coming up." JT smiled. "Except all the senior stuff, and I won't be too into that."

Nadia nodded at the reference to their junior status. "Ah, but what I have planned will make any senior activity look like a day at the library."

JT turned to face her. "What do you mean, Nad?"

Nadia pulled the elastic band out of her hair and shook her head. Her thick red mane tumbled down her shoulders. "You know the big party my father is having next Saturday night?"

JT nodded.

"Well, I decided to invite a few kids from school—ten exactly. I asked my mom and she said I could."

"Really?" JT was surprised to hear that Nadia's parents had said yes to letting Nadia bring her friends to one of their fancy parties. But she was also glad, for her friend's sake, that Mr. and Mrs. Lawrence were back together again and getting along well enough to give a party. They fought more frequently than they got along. Still, fighting or not, they rarely had time for their daughter. JT had no idea how Nadia had managed to get her mother's approval, but just the thought of going to a Lawrence Hollywood party was very exciting. "Oh, Nad, that's great!"

Nadia smiled. At last she had JT under her wing again. She had been on her best behavior for two weeks now, trying to make up for all the social backsliding she had done since that humiliating episode with Denis Daniels at the spring dance. "Glennie and I have been going over the guest list for days. It's important to have people from different crowds, you know, so they mingle." Nadia paused. "Of course I'm inviting you." JT's big puppy eyes grew wide with pleasure. "Timothy Hutton and Burt Reynolds are coming."

"Are you serious? Oh, Nad, that's incredible. Who else are you going to invite?"

Nadia laughed gaily. "Well, we figured John Shephard from the 'Hills' crowd, Marilyn Wells from the artsy kids, for the jocks John Hamill. Maybe Mindy and Lisa," Nadia added, referring to the girls from her own group. "Someone from media class. Like Grady."

"But what about Kristin Sullivan?— I mean, if you're inviting Grady, he'll probably want to bring her. . . ."

Nadia stomped the pavement. "They're not joined at the hip," she said, her temper showing for the first time that day. It still annoyed her. After doing everything in her power to capture the talented Grady, he still had fallen for that sappy midwesterner. Even without Kristin, though, she couldn't imagine him turning down a party like this. No one would.

"Did you hear that Kristin and Monica Miller are going to be in the new Jack Lemmon movie?" JT asked her. "Josh Ross told me in media class that they're both missing school next Friday to shoot."

Nadia gritted her teeth and tried to control herself. She had heard the same thing today at school, and that bit of unwelcome news had made her even more glad that she had convinced (or, rather, threatened, cried, and begged) her mother to let her invite some of her friends to the party. She couldn't stand seeing Kristin and Monica get all that attention while everyone forgot about her. "So, do you think you can come?" Nadia asked.

JT hugged her. "Oh, Nad, how can you even ask that? Of course I'll come. I wouldn't miss it for anything."

Nadia hugged her back. "I can always count on you."

Suddenly JT was distracted by the insistent honking of a horn and a raucous holler. At first she looked intentionally away from the street, thinking it was just some creep making a pass at Nadia. Then she saw the reflection of the silver Porsche in the boutique window. JT felt her knees almost buckle underneath her as the sportscar pulled up at the curb and the driver stuck his head out.

"HEY, CUTIES!" Denis yelled out. At the sound of his voice Nadia whipped around and took a defensive stance. Denis started laughing.

"Denis Daniels, you are such a lowlife," Nadia complained.

"Whoa, whoa ..." Denis called, "I was just saying hi. I mean, you're pretty cute, Nad. JT too."

Nadia looked anything but cute at that moment; in fact, she looked as if she could have eaten Denis alive, but JT's pulse quickened in spite of herself. Denis always had that effect on her. His blue eyes were so sad, so needy. They made her want to throw her arms around him, hug him to her. But she knew that he never thought of her as anything but a friend. She stayed back with Nadia and watched the way the sun glistened off Denis's golden hair.

Denis smiled rougishly and drummed the outside of his car with his fingertips. "So what's happening?"

"What's happening is that you're going to get yourself arrested if you keep up the way you've been lately," Nadia warned fiercely.

"Oh, Nadia, c'mon," Denis teased, "I'm a sweet guy."

"Give me a break," Nadia said without an instant's hesitation. "I haven't seen you at school for about a week."

Denis threw her a kiss. "Miss me, huh?"

He laughed again, but this time JT felt a little sick inside. Denis was the reason she had almost broken with Nadia. She still found it hard to believe that her best friend had deliberately set him up to get caught for smoking dope at school. Of course, it was Denis who had actually gotten in trouble—Nadia had only set the trap. But Denis had taken his revenge by humiliating Nadia with a prank at the spring dance. So he had been suspended again. Now he was supposed to be back, but he was still cutting a lot of school, and everyone said he was using drugs again. At that moment his eyes were red and his expression careless. It broke JT's heart to see him like that.

Almost as if he'd read her mind, Denis turned to her. "Hey, JT, what's new with you?" His tone was suddenly kind and caring.

"Denis, give us both a break and bug off, okay?" Nadia interrupted.

But JT couldn't stop herself; she took a step toward the car. When she put her hand on the window frame Denis reached over and touched her. His casual gesture reverberated through her body as if someone had struck a bell. If only Denis would let her, JT thought, she could save him. She just knew she could. "I'm okay. We've missed you in media class the last few days."

Denis looked away painfully. He took a pair of dark glasses from off his dashboard and put them on. They made him look like some kind of golden-haired gangster. "Yeah, well, man, I've been busy. You know how it is."

JT nodded.

Denis perked up. He looked back at Nadia. "So what are you doing, Lawrence," he goaded, "trying to show off your bod to all the tourists?"

"Don't you wish," Nadia retorted.

JT couldn't stand being in the middle of their antagonism. She began to rattle on nervously, trying to change the subject. "We just took class at the Workout," she chattered. "I was thinking of shopping for something to wear to a party that Nadia's giv ..."

Suddenly JT felt Nadia's long nails dig into her fleshy forearm. She turned to see her friend give her a look that would have scared Mr. T. For a moment JT just stared back.

"Well, give my regards to Sunset," Denis threw out. "See ya around." With a charming smile he revved up his Porsche and sped out into the traffic, causing a Mercedes to slam on its brakes and let him by. JT watched the cloud of exhaust that Denis left behind before turning back to Nadia.

Nadia immediately defended herself. "I'm sorry, JT," she said quickly, but still with some irritation in her voice. "I didn't mean to hurt you. I just had to stop you from telling Denis about my parents' party."

"Why?" JT rubbed her arm. There were two dents from Nadia's fingernails.

"Are you kidding? Denis is really getting bad. I've heard he's hanging out with some incredibly sleazy kids from Hollywood. He would like nothing better than to find out about a party of mine and crash it. My parents would kill me."

JT looked down. Nadia was probably right. "I guess I didn't think," she admitted guiltily.

Nadia decided not to push it. She forced a smile onto her face and looked back toward the shop window. "Don't worry about it," she assured JT. "Come on, you're going to go in and try on that jumpsuit, and if it doesn't look fabulous I am going to take you up and down Rodeo Drive until we find something that does. Okay?"

JT looked down the street for one more moment; then she turned back to Nadia and sighed. "Okay."

7

THE FRISBEE SEEMED TO PAUSE, HOVERING IN MIDAIR AS IF deciding which way to turn. Josh leapt for it, his strong legs lifting him off the Sunset High lawn at least several feet. He was almost blinded by the bright noontime sun.

"All right!" yelled Eddie Santiago. He had his shirt tied over his head like an Arab sheik. "It's Josh Ross of the Frisbee all-stars."

Eddie and Kristin laughed as Josh tossed the Frisbee toward Monica. She was holding out her hands and scampering for it like a basketball guard. Grady stood further off, not budging, just moodily skimming the grass with the heel of his old hiking boot. Monica caught the Frisbee and then tossed it off. The disk took an unpredictable spin, skirting away from Kristin and Eddie and heading for Grady.

Catching it deftly, if unenthusiastically, Grady flipped it back at Monica, but the disk curved more toward Josh. Monica raced him for it, but Josh sidestepped across the grass until he was within reach again. Then he jumped—stretching his tanned arm, the tips of his fingers making contact with the hard plastic. It wasn't until after he jumped, when he was in the air, that Josh realized that it would not be an easy landing. But that was all right. Josh never liked having the easy way for anything.

"All right, Ross!!!"

Josh felt the bottoms of his running shoes slip on the grass and his ankles crumple. He threw his body into it, the way he used to slide stealing bases in Little League and then, at the last second, saw that Monica, who'd been rushing alongside him to catch the Frisbee, was no more than two feet away. Josh tried to shift his body, but it was too late. He slid gently into Monica with the flat of his back and they both went tumbling down. Josh landed on his side and lifted his head.

"You okay?" he asked, immediately putting a hand out. It landed on Monica's bare calf.

Monica rolled onto her back and leaned on her elbows. She began to giggle. "Yeah, I'll live."

Her cheeks were infused with a healthy pink glow. Wisps of dark hair fell over her forehead, and her dimples were showing. Looking warmly into Josh's face, she seemed to be challenging him in some way.

Josh sat up. His glasses were slightly askew and he readjusted them. He wasn't sure he was seeing correctly. For weeks he had been trying to get Monica's attention, but with no luck. She had consistently treated him like a little brother. But today there was far more than brotherly affection in her expression.

"You sure?" He removed his hand, suddenly very aware that it was resting on her leg. His heart had just started to thump.

Monica sat up cross-legged and examined her knees for grass stains. "No damage." She smiled brightly. She did it again, gave him a flirty look. "How about you?"

Josh smiled. "Me? It takes more than that to hurt me."

"Well, me too," Monica teased. She pushed back her dark bangs and readjusted her sweatshirt. They both offered each other their hands and managed to pull themselves up.

"Hey, c'mon. This is delay of game," Eddie yelled. "Let's see that Frisbee out here...."

Josh flipped the Frisbee back, feeling a little self-conscious.

"You're really good at this," Monica said, watching him.

Josh grinned. "Yeah, I know, great hands. Took years to develop."

Monica laughed and Josh suddenly found himself feeling ten feet tall. He prided himself in being sensitive and aware of other people, and generally he knew when a girl was interested in him and when she wasn't. Until now he had been positive that Monica never gave him a second thought. Only yesterday he had told himself it was time to forget about her. But today there was something new in her face, something that gave him hope.

Monica put her hands in her pockets and smiled. "You should show me how to do that. Maybe sometime ... Hey! Oh, here it comes."

The Frisbee was heading their way again, and this time Monica managed to clap her hands around it before Josh could react. She took a few springy leaps and then launched it into the air. In her print overalls she looked like a beautiful street urchin. Josh wanted to run over and throw his arms around her, or make her laugh so he could see her dimples again. When Monica caught him staring, she looked down a little coyly, but then smiled back.

"Pretty lame, I know," Monica admitted.

"Not bad," Josh countered. "You're really graceful."

"C'mon, I'm a klutz."

Backing up and wiping his forehead with the cuff of his rugby shirt, Josh wondered if this was too good to be true. He couldn't help but wonder why Monica had suddenly changed toward him. Maybe she just had spring fever, he warned himself. It was one of those steamy almost-summer days that made him feel as if he wanted to really cut loose. Maybe that was all Monica was responding to.

"Eddie, this is headed right at you," Kristin yelled from across the field.

Eddie dove after the Frisbee, his makeshift headpiece flying off as he landed in a comic somersault. With a moan he collapsed on his back like a dead man.

"Hey, Eddie, are you all right?" Josh yelled.

"Ohhhh," Eddie moaned, "this is worse than last semester's chemistry final."

"I think it's all over for Eddie," giggled Monica. The group ran up to him.

"He left us without even taking the shirt on his back," kidded Kristin, picking up Eddie's shirt and dropping it on his face. Even Grady smiled.

"Hey, nature man," teased Josh, picking up some leaves from a nearby bush and scattering them over Eddie.

"Now, wait a minute," Eddie protested, sitting up. "I'll take a lot of abuse, but please don't make me go through any of that nature stuff again."

Josh and Eddie laughed knowingly, and Eddie turned to explain to the others.

"Do you know what this guy did to me last weekend?" he said, gesturing to Josh with his long, bony hand. "He drove me about eighty miles to take a two-hour hike in the woods. We sat and looked at this stream for about an hour, talked to the deer. Not quite what I'd call an 'E' ticket at Disneyland."

Josh smiled. Eddie's good-natured teasing didn't bother him. Josh made no excuses for who he was or how he liked to spend his time. He was proud of it.

"Eddie kept trying to tell jokes to the fish," Josh explained. "They were about as responsive as everybody else who hears his jokes."

Eddie batted Josh with the Frisbee. "More responsive," he admitted.

Everyone laughed except Grady.

Without warning, Eddie tossed the Frisbee right

at his friend's stomach. Grady caught it and flicked it away, obviously still out of sorts.

"Hey, Eddie," Grady recalled, "aren't we supposed to meet Matt and everybody up at the student store today?"

Eddie tapped himself on the head with the Frisbee. "Oh, yeah, it's senioritis gone wild. Order slips for caps and gowns."

"K, you want to come too?" Grady asked dejectedly, turning toward her.

Kristin put her hands in her jeans pockets and joined him. She bumped him with her shoulder. "It's just caps and gowns, Grady," she teased, "not the firing squad."

Grady looked a little embarrassed. He gave her a playful swat and rested his arm around her.

Eddie was pulling his shirt back on, already starting back up the slope. "You guys should come too." He gestured to Monica and Josh. "You can find out the secret of our class's superior reputation."

"I think I know too much already," Josh cracked back. "Anyway, I want to stay out here." He took a deep breath of the hot, deserty air, unable to bear the thought of going indoors one second earlier than necessary.

"Monica, you want to come?" asked Kristin.

Monica looked back at Josh, then checked her Mickey Mouse watch. "I think I'll stay out here too. I have to be in the swim-gym fifth period," she said casually, referring to the famous Sunset High swimming pool that was topped with a roll-away floor to convert it into a gym. The old building was close by, just on the other side of the tennis courts.

Kristin hesitated for a moment. "Okay," she said finally. "See you all later." She paused to let Grady and Eddie get a few yards ahead, then leaning back to Josh, she whispered, "Karen Small and John Shephard just told me they're coming to the party. And Eddie's sister, Elena. So we're up to thirty already."

"I got at least five more yeses this morning," Josh whispered, "so that makes it thirty-five. Do you think he knows?"

"No."

Kristin glanced around. Grady had just turned away from Eddie and was waiting for her. " 'Bye," she said quickly.

Monica and Josh waved as the trio headed toward the low row of stucco classrooms. Suddenly very aware of being alone, they sat on the grass for a moment in awkward silence. They smiled at each other. Josh was stretched out, leaning back on his hands. Monica hugged her knees against her chest. They watched a group of sunbathers and a spontaneous touch football game further down the lawn.

"So you really took Eddie on a two-hour nature hike?" Monica said at last.

Josh looked over at her. It was the first time she had asked him anything about himself. He had only gotten to know her at all because she was a good friend of Kristin's. Of course they had been in the same biology class all year, and he had definitely noticed her—knew that she had been a child actress and all that—and really thought she was good-looking. But it wasn't until he danced a long slow dance with her at the spring dance several weeks before that his feelings had developed. Something about the vulnerable way she slipped into his arms ... the way she always seemed to be a little scared or on her guard, as if she were trying to act tougher than she really was. Even now he felt it. He wondered why, after they had hung around each other casually for the last few weeks, she was suddenly showing interest in him. Monica inched closer and Josh's stomach flipflopped.

"You should have seen us," he answered her. "It was great. We'd gone all that way to get away from civilization and Eddie brought a portable radio." He turned to her. Her shoulder was brushing against his. "Are you going to Grady's surprise party?"

Monica's face suddenly clouded. "I don't think I can." She nervously pulled a clump of grass and scattered the blades over her clear plastic shoes. "I think I have to go somewhere for business. My acting, you know."

Josh nodded. He knew other kids at Sunset who pursued professional entertainment careers. They all had a kind of grown-up, tired look in their eyes. He looked over and saw that look now in Monica's face. Moments before she had been as carefree as a toddler. The change made him a little sad.

"Is it for that movie you and Kristin are going to be in? I heard about that. It's pretty exciting."

Monica smiled, less tense. "Yeah, it's great. But the night of the party I have to do something else. It has to do with this TV series I'm being considered for."

"Oh." Josh didn't really understand why Monica would have to do something for her TV series on a Saturday night. "That's too bad. I'm sure Kristin really wants you to come."

Monica got that adult look again. "Well, you know how it is."

"Yeah."

They sat in silence. Twice Monica looked over at him and seemed to be about to say something, but didn't. Finally the bell rang, announcing the end of lunch, and Josh stood up.

"Josh . . ."

Josh felt Monica's hand on his arm. She stood up and looked into his face. Her skin looked so smooth, and her dark hair fell in uneven wisps. He fought the urge to reach up and touch her cheek with his hand. "Yes?"

Monica laughed, a little nervously. "Are you busy this weekend?"

Josh was unable to answer for a second. He was unprepared for a question as inviting as that. He felt his mouth turn up in a huge smile. "Not really. Why?"

Monica spoke quickly. "I'm kind of behind in biology, because I missed a few days in March, and Groener wants me to do some kind of nature study as a make-up project." She paused, looking for a reaction.

Josh waited for her to finish.

"So, I wondered if maybe you could help me. He's so hard, and you're so good in his class." She gave a flirtatious smile again. "I thought it might be fun going on a nature trip ... like with Eddie."

"I hope you're not as hopeless in the outdoors as Eddie."

Monica reacted to his playfulness with a real smile, not a consciously flirtatious one like before. "I make no promises."

Josh looked at her. He could still remember the smell of her hair when he danced with her—like some kind of wildflower.

"How about Sunday? I know some great tide pools out in Malibu."

"Tide pools?"

"These sort of rocky places at the beach where there's a lot of really interesting sea life. Do you think Groener would go for that?"

Monica nodded enthusiastically. "Sounds perfect. Let me give you my phone number."

"Okay." Josh looked around for something to write on. He had stowed his books in his locker before lunch. As Monica took out a pen, he decided to hold out his hand. "Write it here. I'll try not to wash it off before I get home."

Monica held his hand gently, writing with a ballpoint pen. Her touch was light and delicate. "There." She started toward the swim-gym. "Will you call me?"

"Sure."

"I'll see you Sunday, then." Monica walked further off and waved. "Thanks."

Josh waved back and watched her go. He had no idea why she had suddenly changed toward him. But he didn't care. He was absolutely crazy about her.

8

THE SILVER PORSCHE TORE DOWN RESIDENTIAL REXFORD Drive, weaving dangerously from side to side. Kristin could just make out Denis Daniels's blond hair and handsome profile in the driver's seat. She grabbed her father as the car flew past.

"Slow down! There are children around here!" shouted Dr. Sullivan, his hands cupped over his mouth.

Kristin had never seen her father so angry; even the funny bald spot on the top of his head was turning red. Shaking his head, he hiked up his sweat pants and sat down on the curb. His jaw was clenched, and he slapped his fist into his open palm.

Kristin sat down next to him. "Dad, cool it. Remember what you're always telling your patients?"

Her father was a heart specialist. He was always telling his patients to relax. Kristin reached up and massaged his damp neck.

"That Daniels kid is driving me crazy. Last week

he came this close to hitting a little boy on a bike. He's going to kill somebody in that stupid car."

Kristin sighed and stretched out her long legs. Denis Daniels lived on the corner of Rexford and Lomitas, in a red brick mansion just a block up from her much smaller house. This was the second time her father had blown up about his reckless driving.

"I'd like to get my hands on that kid," Dr. Sullivan muttered.

Kristin looked down the palm-tree–lined street past the huge homes protected by hedges and fancy security gates. Denis and his Porsche were long gone.

"I keep reading how his parents care so much about young people. So where are they when it comes to their own son?"

"Dad ..." Kristin tried to soothe him. She had to admit that her father's outburst was justified, but she hated raised voices and angry confrontations. The last few weeks her father had been growing more and more irritable. The slightest thing would set him off.

"I read one article that called his mother 'America's Favorite Mom.' She's not my favorite mom, that's for sure," Dr. Sullivan complained.

"I'm sure the Danielses aren't around very much, with their show and all," reasoned Kristin. Denis's mom was the star of the popular "Deann Daniels Show," and his father was a network executive.

"That's no excuse."

Kristin sighed and faced her father. "Dad, forget it. Let's jog. Come on, it'll make you feel better."

He finally patted her shoulder and stood up. "Okay. I'm just afraid he's going to run somebody over one of these days."

"I know. But there's not much we can do about it now."

Dr. Sullivan nodded and smiled at Kristin. He began a slow trot. Kristin ran a little ahead of him on the street, just next to the curb. Soon they were panting side by side, crossing Sunset Boulevard and heading up into the hills.

Kristin looked over at her father as they ran. "Any new famous patients?" she asked, hoping for a playful response. When they'd first moved to Beverly Hills, her father had been thrilled every time someone in the movie business had come into his office.

Dr. Sullivan just shrugged.

"How about that guy who reads the medical books and then decides he has everything he's read about?" Usually that topic was good for a few jokes. Not today. Her father stared straight ahead, his expression preoccupied, his square face stern.

It concerned Kristin to see her father so tense. The Sullivan family had moved to Beverly Hills so he could join a new prestigious medical practice. At first he had seemed to adjust easily to the new environment, more easily than she. But recently he was starting to show signs of wear. He worked longer hours, lost his temper easily, looked worn despite his Southern California tan.

Running past the Beverly Hills Hotel, up Benedict Canyon, Kristin wondered if her father was catching what she thought of as the "Beverly Hills disease"—the desperate drive for success that seemed to take over some people. She saw it in Monica, who was becoming so consumed by her acting career that she thought nothing of using Josh to help her with biology. She saw it in Grady, where the goal of getting into a top Ivy League school seemed to obscure everything else. She saw it in so many kids at school, high school students who felt that they *had* to wear the best clothes or drive the most expensive cars. Kristin knew that all that agonizing wasn't worth it, though. Nothing was.

The canyon road grew steeper, and Dr. Sullivan slowed to a walk, wiping the sweat off his freckled skin with his terry wristband. Kristin stopped running too.

"Dad, why don't you and Mom get away from here for a few days?" she suggested casually. Deep down, Kristin was afraid that her parents' strong marriage was starting to suffer from the strain. Just last night her father's decision to work late rather than attend a meeting at her brother's school had caused a terrible argument. "I think you need to relax or something."

Her father stared up at a plane that was skywriting in long, even loops. After a moment, he smiled and turned to her. "Who do you think you are, handing out advice like that? Me?"

They both laughed. He dropped his arm over her shoulder.

"I'm serious," Kristin continued. "It's bad enough

I have a boyfriend I have to cheer up all the time. If you poop out on me, I don't think I can take it."

He made a teasing face. "Poop out? I would never poop out on you, honey."

They walked slowly up the hill, past modern redwood houses and steep ivied slopes. "You know what I mean."

"Yes, I know what you mean." He paused and started down in a slow, bumpy jog. "You know I have this patient who offered us his ranch in Santa Barbara next weekend. Maybe we should all go."

"Next weekend?"

"Oh, that's right. You have your surprise party for Grady."

"Dad, why don't you take Mom and Shawn and go without me? I'm perfectly capable of taking care of myself for one weekend."

"I don't know. We're the only people in this crazy town that don't have a burglar alarm and a security gate. I'm beginning to wonder if there isn't a reason everybody here is so paranoid. I don't want anybody stealing you while I'm away."

Kristin could tell his concern was real, but his voice was light and teasing—more like the way he usually was with her. She lightly poked him in the ribs as they ran back down Benedict toward Sunset Boulevard.

"I bet Monica could sleep over on Friday after we shoot the movie, and then I could sleep over at her house on Saturday after Grady's party. Anyway, then I wouldn't be alone at night."

They stopped and waited for the traffic light

before crossing Sunset. "That's not a bad idea. Are you sure you'll be okay?"

"Dad, don't you trust me?"

"Well ..." He smiled mischievously. "Yes, I do. It's a good idea. I know your mother would love to get away for a few days. I hear it's beautiful up there."

"Good. Race you home, old man?"

He gave her a challenging stare. "You're one nervy kid, you know that?" Then, as soon as the light changed he took off, taking her by surprise. Kristin sprinted to catch up.

They flew back down Sunset turning back onto Rexford toward home, but when they got to the corner of Lomitas Avenue, Dr. Sullivan suddenly stopped. Standing in front of the Daniels mansion, he looked up the long driveway. His expression was tense again.

"Why are you stopping, Dad?"

"I think I'm going to pay my neighbor a little visit."

"What!"

He was already walking up the driveway to the black metal gate before Kristin could reason with him. She rushed up to him and grabbed his arm, but he had already pushed the button on the small intercom box.

"Dad, come on. Don't be ridiculous," Kristin urged, pulling on his shirt. She recognized the look on her father's face from his old neighborhood meetings back in St. Cloud. Clearly he wanted to face Denis's parents and make a complaint.

Kristin was incredibly embarrassed by the whole thing and tried to pry him away.

"Dad, let's go."

He was unbudgeable. Kristin was just starting down the driveway on her own when a female voice came over the intercom.

"Can I help you both?" asked the voice, which had some kind of European accent. Kristin froze. She was stuck. Mortified, she turned back as her father spoke into the metal intercom box.

"I am Dr. Sullivan, and this is my daughter, Kristin," he announced stiffly. "I'd like to talk to either Mr. or Mrs. Daniels about something important." Kristin wrapped her arms around herself and stared at the ground.

The woman questioned him further to make sure that he was a legitimate neighbor. Finally the gate opened electronically. Head down, Kristin followed her father along the large circular driveway and up to the front door.

The Daniels' house was a two-story brick with large white columns in the front, sort of a California imitation of a Southern plantation house. The yard was immaculately manicured and covered with colorful flowers. As they reached the door it was opened by a plain elderly woman in a white uniform.

"Good afternoon," she said formally. Kristin decided that her accent was German or Austrian. "Mr. Daniels will be with you in a moment."

She led the Sullivans into a small study just off the main hall. The room was furnished in early American antiques and everything was color-coordinated, from the pillows on the loveseat to the books on the rolltop desk. Even the insides of the window frames were lined in a matching rose color. It was an interior decorator's showpiece.

Kristin felt very out of place in her sweaty running clothes. She was trying to decide whether or not to sit down when Mr. Daniels appeared in the doorway. He smiled and extended a hand to her father.

"Hello, I'm Steven Daniels," he said robustly.

"Ken Sullivan. This is my daughter, Kristin."

Mr. Daniels shook both their hands. He was tall and handsome, with the same rugged good looks as his son. Unlike Denis's, however, his hair was silver. Mr. Daniels wore a starched pink shirt, dark slacks, and loafers that Kristin had learned to identify as Guccis. He glanced at his Rolex watch.

"I don't mean to be rude," Daniels said politely, "but I have a limo coming to take me to the airport any minute."

"I understand," Dr. Sullivan answered. He shifted.

Daniels filled in the pause expertly. "You must live in that two-story at the other end of the block, across from Harry and Thelma. It's terrible how nobody in L.A. knows their neighbors. I appreciate your stopping by to say hello." Before Kristin knew it, he was subtly ushering them out, and she and her father found themselves at the front door again.

Dr. Sullivan quickly spoke up. "Actually, the reason I came by is to talk to you about your son Denis."

Mr. Daniels's charming manner dropped for an instant. His mouth bunched up and his eyes narrowed. Then he regained control and smiled again.

"Your son drives up and down this street much too fast," Kristin's father continued. "He's going to hurt somebody if he's not careful."

"How do you know it's my son?" Steven Daniels challenged his neighbor.

Kristin's father cleared his throat. "I don't know of another Porsche like that on this block."

"How do you know the driver lives on this block? Or if it is Denis's car, maybe someone else is driving it." Mr. Daniels's voice was steely.

"It's Denis," Dr. Sullivan insisted. "Would you please tell him that the neighbors are very upset."

"Dr. Sullivan," Daniels said coolly, "I could just as easily tell you that it was your daughter here who was causing trouble. I am a busy man with a reputation to protect. I would appreciate it if you would keep your hearsay and your ideas about who is upsetting the neighborhood to yourself. If you have facts, I will be glad to hear them. In the meantime, I have faith in my son. Now, if you'll excuse me, I have to be ready to leave in a few minutes." He held open the door. "Good-bye."

Dr. Sullivan left without a word. Kristin walked by his side the remainder of the block home.

"Dad, just forget about it. It's not that big a deal."

"I can't believe he would lie like that! How could he not know what that jerk kid of his is doing?"

"I don't know," Kristin mumbled as she reached their house. All she knew was that she saw that look again on the face of Steven Daniels—that Beverly Hills look—and it gave her the creeps.

9

Warren Taylor called. Will call back.

It was Sunday morning, and Monica stared at the little pink memo that the maid had taped to her bedroom door.

Will call back!!!

She read the words over again several times. Warren had actually called her and was going to call back! The young actor *had* to be interested in her.... There was no other way to interpret the message. Monica fell back on her bed in a daze and giggled. Her spirits soared, and she felt as light and giddy as a helium balloon.

"Monica," her mother called out, "do you want a croissant?"

Monica tried to come back down to earth. But she'd never really left the clouds ever since she'd found out about the movie, since she'd met Warren.

"Okay."

"It's on the kitchen table."

Monica wanted a few more minutes alone. She

jumped up, and stood in front of the mirror, posing, imagining the photo of herself—star of the new series "Laurie and Me"— and hunky boyfriend Warren Taylor. The *People* magazine spread would show her and Warren wearing funny hats, relaxing together off the set, maybe feeding each other homemade pasta. Her mother would frame the pictures and put them in her office along with her other famous clients. Monica was just pulling her hair away from her face, imagining her title shot for "Laurie and Me," when she heard the doorbell.

"Does somebody want to answer the door?" her mom called.

"I'll get it," Monica yelled, racing out of her bedroom. It was probably Josh. In her rapture over Warren she had almost forgotten her Sunday-morning date to go to the beach with Josh. Monica flew down the hall and swung open the front door.

Josh Ross stood in front of her.

"Hi."

"Hi."

"It's a perfect day to go to the beach." Josh gestured to the cloudless sky.

He was wearing canvas hiking shorts, a baggy dark green tee-shirt, and jogging shoes with no socks. His curly hair was not quite dry, and he looked like he had spent his entire Saturday in the sun. A pair of sunglasses was tucked into the neck of his tee-shirt.

For a moment Monica was caught off guard.

She had never seen him without his glasses before. His greenish-brown eyes looked so naked, so intense, as he stared back at her, his gaze steady and knowing. She shifted, feeling uncomfortable. What was it about Josh that gave her the impression he knew more about her than he let on? Something about those probing eyes ... Monica stiffened and looked away. Josh remained, his stance as relaxed and self-assured as ever.

"Ready to go?" he asked easily.

"Just give me a sec." Monica rushed back down the hall to fetch her clear plastic flats and a sweatshirt to wear over her sleeveless tee-shirt and army surplus pants. She tied the sweatshirt over her bare shoulders.

When she came back Josh was kneeling to one side of the doorway, examining a bird of paradise plant with the tenderness of a good doctor. There was something about the composed look on his face, the strong slope of his shoulder, that moved her. He seemed absorbed, and as Monica watched, he touched the flower as if it were the most valuable thing in the world. Unaware that she had returned, he ran his hand gently along the sides of the stalk.

"I'm ready," Monica finally said, anxious to get down to business.

He looked up and smiled warmly, finally tearing himself away from the beautiful plant. "I brought you a couple of books to help you write up your report later, so you don't have to bring paper or anything."

"Great. Thanks."

"Let's get going."

Monica followed Josh out the front driveway until she saw a junky old van parked along the curb. Josh was headed right for it. As Monica got closer she saw "Solar Systems by Ross" painted on the side. Underneath, in smaller script, was an address in nearby Culver City.

The van was parked between a Mercedes station wagon and a Fiat sports car. The only vehicle like it on the block was the pickup across the street, which belonged to the pool cleaner. Josh opened the door for her. The front seat was high off the ground, and Monica had to hold on to the door frame to pull herself up. She felt Josh's hands gently guiding her waist as she slid in. A pile of books were scattered around the floor at her feet. Monica pulled her legs up and sat Indian-style. Josh jogged around to the other side and lifted himself up with one graceful jump.

"If you want, you can toss that stuff in the back," he told her as he adjusted the side-view mirror.

"That's okay."

Josh put his sunglasses on and tossed a wrench into a toolbox behind him. The back of the van was filled with ladders, rope, something that looked like small mirrors, plastic pipe, and more tools.

"This is my dad's van. It was a good thing he let me use it. I don't have a car," Josh explained with a smile. He started the van and expertly turned it around.

Monica pulled her knees up to her chest and watched him. "What does your dad do?"

"He puts in solar panels." Josh stuck a tape into an inexpensive deck. The music was a kind of space-age flute. "What does your dad do?"

"My dad?" For a moment Monica was thrown off guard. She never talked about her father. "I don't know," she found herself admitting. "I mean, my parents have been divorced since I was a baby. I don't really remember my father at all."

Josh looked at her until the light changed, and Monica got that strange feeling again. She felt that, even with the dark glasses on, he was looking right into her.

"My mom's an agent," she said quickly, looking away. "She represents a lot of big stars ... and a few not-so-big stars, like me."

Josh smiled. "My mom works too. She's the nurse at Sunset."

"At school, you mean? Your mom is the Sunset High nurse?" Monica didn't mean to sound so shocked, but she was surprised that Josh was so open about it. Most kids in Beverly Hills would be incredibly embarrassed by something like that.

"Just in the mornings," he said confidently. "She uses her maiden name, so I guess not that many people know she's my mom. She's the original liberated woman." He laughed. "See, we live in Culver City, so that's why I get to go to school there."

Monica nodded. Because it was the only school in such an extraordinarily wealthy community,

Sunset was one of the best public high schools in the country. The only way to enroll there was to be a Beverly Hills resident or have a parent who was on staff.

They drove west on Sunset Boulevard, leaving behind Beverly Hills and the hot inland smog. Soon they were winding through Pacific Palisades, looking out at the rugged cliffs and enjoying the cooler air. Monica could smell the ocean.

"A lot of people don't even know that there are tide pools in Malibu," Josh explained as they drove.

Monica nodded. She had certainly never known that. Her own uncle lived out there, yet she had never thought of Malibu as anything but another Beverly Hills that just happened to be next to the ocean.

"How did you find out?"

"I just found them one day last year. There was a party at John Shephard's folks' beach house and I went exploring. It's sort of a trek to get to the pools." He laughed. "By the time I got back it was so late everybody else had gone home."

Monica laughed too. She stuck her head out the window and felt the wonderful rush of clean air against her face. They turned onto the Pacific Coast Highway and headed north along the water's edge.

"It's such a great day," Monica said, staring out at the expanse of water. Something about the easy movement of the waves, the pure blue color, was so peaceful. She took off her sweatshirt and stretched her arms over her head.

Josh drove up the highway a little ways further, finally pulling off the side of the road onto a narrow shoulder. There were two other trucks parked there, both filled with fishing gear. "This is it."

Monica looked around. The area was fairly deserted, and before her was not a flat, sandy beach but a steep cliff that led down to the water.

Josh noticed her concern. "Don't worry," he said, locking up the van. "It looks a lot worse than it is. There's a path ... sort of."

"I'm beginning to see what Eddie was talking about."

Josh grinned. "Sometimes the best places are the hardest ones to get to."

He led the way to the edge of the cliff. He paused for a moment, taking in the cool sea air, then started to climb down. Monica hesitated at the top. It was very steep.

"Come on," Josh called from a little ways below. In one motion he grabbed his tee-shirt and pulled it off, exposing a tan and finely muscled chest. Staring down at him, Monica felt her cheeks warm and her breath quicken. She tried not to look at him as he stuck the tee-shirt in the waistband of his shorts and waited for her.

Monica started to slowly back down the hill, holding on to roots and rocks for support. Most of the way she found indentations that could be used as steps. But the flat plastic bottom of her shoes gave little traction, and she was constantly grabbing whatever she could to keep from slipping. She made sure Josh stayed just slightly ahead of her, but he kept stopping and looking back, checking to see that she was all right. Monica found herself grabbing the roots so tightly that her hands were starting to burn.

At the bottom was a drop of about six feet to the sand. Josh jumped down easily, but she halted. It looked like a long way.

Josh held his arms out and stood beneath her. "Just lower yourself down. I'll catch you."

Monica swallowed nervously, staring at his outstretched arms and bare chest. She felt very warm all of a sudden and looked around, trying to spot another way. But the rocks were too far apart for her short stride. "Okay." Her voice came out a little shaky. Facing the cliff, she lowered herself slowly until she let go of a strong bush and allowed her body to drop.

She gasped as Josh caught her. She had her back to him, and with his arms wrapped tight around her, she could feel his smooth sun-baked skin against the side of her cheek. Her heart was beating very fast, and it was hard to think. Slowly he relaxed his hold, and she turned around to face him.

"You all right?" His voice sounded a little odd now too. Breathless. They stood very close.

Looking up into his face, Monica felt almost dizzy. It was the climb, she told herself. It was only the climb. "Uh-huh," she answered in a whispery voice. "I'm fine." Making herself break away, she rushed down to the water.

Josh cleared his throat. "The pools are over

this way." He pointed to some low rocks that were scattered in the shallow water.

Monica joined him, keeping her distance. Unlike the way she had felt at the Frisbee game a few days before, she didn't trust herself enough to get too close. She wanted everything under control. Josh held out his hand as he started to step across the rocks, but she didn't take it.

"We're lucky. It's really low tide," he said, crouching down and looking into the water. Glancing over his shoulder, Monica saw that the tiny pools were filled with round creatures of various colors. "Watch." Josh poked his finger into the middle of one of the creatures. All the wavy tentacles closed around him.

Monica moved in. She was fascinated. "What is that?"

"Just a sea anemone. I figured that's what you could write your paper on."

Monica stuck her finger in another anemone. It tickled as it wrapped its wavy arms around her. She laughed. "That feels so weird."

"I know."

Monica took off her shoe and poked one with her toe. She laughed again. "Does it think I'm food?"

"Yup. That's its mouth. See, it attaches itself to a rock and then gathers food as it swims by."

Josh got up and moved farther out, stepping easily from rock to rock. Small waves rolled over the tops of his feet. He pulled off his shoes and tossed them up onto the sand. Monica did the same and rolled her baggy pants up above her knees as they waded into deeper water.

Josh leaned across a crevice and looked down. It was filled with all kinds of sea life, not just anemones but also silvery fish, pieces of coral, and some creatures that looked like cucumbers.

Monica listened as he pointed out different species and explained how they moved or what they ate. Her body relaxed under the hot sun. The salty air felt good against her skin, and the water cooled her legs and feet every time a wave came up. "Oh, look!" She got down on her knees, having spotted something that looked like a shell with legs. It was crawling across a rock a few feet away.

"Oh, wow, it's a hermit crab."

"What's that?"

Josh leaned over. "It takes an anemone's shell and moves in till it gets too big. Sort of a crab condo."

"Hey," giggled Monica. "If this is Malibu, that shell must be prime real estate."

Josh laughed. Then in a suddenly urgent voice, he cried, "Monica!"

She looked up just in time to see a large wave heading right for her. Before she could move, it crashed down on her and her knees slipped off the rock and into the water. By the time the wave had passed she was soaked all the way up to her waist. She looked back at Josh, who'd been tossed all the way into the open water. He stood there in it up to his hips, looking totally surprised. She started to laugh.

"What's so funny?"

Monica couldn't stop giggling. "You. Your shirt."

He looked around and finally saw his tee-shirt floating away. He swam after it and tossed it back to her.

She caught it and the water sprayed in her face. "Thanks a lot."

"Anytime. Hey," he enticed, coming toward her with his arms outstretched, "the water feels pretty good."

"I bet it does. Forget it."

Josh grabbed one end of the wet tee-shirt, and they began a playful tug-o'-war. He relaxed for a moment, as if he were giving up, and then caught her off guard with a hard tug.

Monica shrieked as she felt her feet give way, and she plopped ungracefully into the water. Now soaked up to her armpits, she wanted revenge. Swinging the wet tee-shirt menacingly, Monica started to go after Josh. The water splashed all around her as she waded through it. "You're not fair!"

He grinned and ran up onto the sand. "Did I ever tell you I was?"

She caught his ankle, and he spilled onto the sand, pulling her down next to him. Monica dug into the damp sand with her hands, enjoying its grainy coolness between her fingers. A layer of sand coated one leg and half of her arm. Her head fell back, and she rolled onto her side, panting and laughing at the same time.

"Do you know what I've always wanted to do?" she asked impulsively.

Josh scooted up next to her, listening as if whatever she said was the most important thing in the world. "What?"

"Make a sand castle."

"You've never made a sand castle?" he asked incredulously. "You grew up in Southern California and you've never made a sand castle?"

"Well, maybe when I was really little. But I don't remember it."

Immediately Josh started to dig. "This is a serious problem. I happen to have been a champion sand castle builder. Of my seven brothers and sisters and me, I was always the best."

On her knees, Monica scooped sand into a lumpy wall. Her damp hair fell in her eyes, and she swept it away with a sandy hand. "You have seven brothers and sisters?"

"I wouldn't lie about something like that," Josh said, turning around and starting on a central tower. "How about you?"

"Just me ... and my mom."

"That's probably better in some ways. I'm second to the oldest. There was always a little kid to help take care of. That's how come I'm so good at sand castles."

A little while later, Monica made notches in the top of the tower and backed up to look. "That's the dungeon."

Josh nodded approvingly.

"It's weird," Monica remarked. "I really don't remember ever doing this. There are so many little-kid things I never did. Sometimes now I have these terrible urges to go on the swings in the park—you know, stuff like that. Isn't that dumb?"

"What's dumb about it?"

"Well, I don't fit in the seats, for one thing."

Josh didn't laugh. "No, really, what's dumb about it?"

"I don't know. I guess I'm too old."

Josh patted the castle wall, smoothing it with the side of his hand. "I don't think you can ever be too old to do stuff like that."

"Really?" Monica sat back thoughtfully. "You know, I think even when I was really little I thought I was too old." She started to turn away, but Josh lightly touched her foot.

"How come?"

Monica hugged one knee and looked out over the ocean. "I guess because I was always this little pro. All those years when I was on 'The Twain Family,' everybody expected me to be a little grownup. I remember one time I was on the set and there was this puppy—he was in one of the scenes. Between takes I chased the puppy around and played with him, and eventually we knocked over a light. So my tutor gave me this lecture about how I was luckier than other kids because I got to be an actress, and how I had this responsibility as a result to act like a grownup. That was what they wanted me to be . . . so that's how I acted." She sighed. "It's weird. I haven't thought about that for a long time."

Josh was listening intently. Something about the way he looked at her made Monica want to keep talking.

"It must be great," Monica said, gazing back at him. "I mean, having lots of brothers and sisters."

"Sometimes." He smiled. "Sometimes it's a real pain. Why do you think it would be great?"

Monica took a handful of sand and slowly let it trickle down her leg. "I guess because you'd always have somebody else to think about. Sometimes I feel as if the only important thing is my career. So when I don't get a part or something, it's more than just a disappointment—I don't have anything. Umm ... It's hard to explain."

Josh moved closer. She could feel the heat radiating from his skin even though he wasn't touching her. "You're doing great," he said. "Keep going."

"And if you were part of this big family, you'd have to just be yourself," Monica continued quickly. "I spend all this time trying to figure out what my mom and everybody else expects of me. I'm always worried that Mom is going to be disappointed if I don't make it. Maybe if I had lots of brothers and sisters it wouldn't matter so much, since all her hopes wouldn't rest on me." She looked away, embarrassed at having said so much. "I just need to be tougher, I guess."

"Why would you want to be tough?"

Monica paused. Josh was leaning toward her, and she had a sudden urge to snuggle up against him, to rest her face against his chest. But she couldn't let that happen. She just couldn't.

"Because I'm supposed to be ... because that's how you make it," Monica said. She felt a surprising catch in her throat. "Because my mom expects it." She bit her lip after she said it.

Josh's steady gaze searched her face. He moved closer, and Monica felt her face grow warm. Everything seemed to stop for a minute. She thought he was going to kiss her. But he didn't. Instead, he gently touched her cheek and brushed her wet hair away from her eyes. Monica's heart was pounding as hard as the waves.

She looked away. She was so scared all of a sudden that she almost covered her eyes with her sandy hands. She couldn't believe that she had just said so much to Josh. And what about the way she felt inside? So full and warm. This feeling was very different from the lighthearted infatuation she felt for Warren. This was something much deeper and more solid.

Warren. Monica thought about him and knew she was blushing. It was only a few hours ago that she had read his note and been so excited. What was happening to her? She looked over at Josh's strong profile and moved away. This was crazy. She had to fight whatever was going on here. She had to get the afternoon back on track. This was a detour that she was not supposed to take.

Monica stood up and brushed the sand off her legs. "I guess we'd better look at the tide pools some more. I mean, I am supposed to write a paper." She smiled nervously and took a few steps back. Her pulse started to return to normal.

Josh stood up too. There was an extra pink glow

under his healthy tan. "Oh, yeah. Right." He walked her back over to the rocks.

They both crouched down and looked into the water. But every so often their eyes would meet again, and Josh's lecture would stop. Each time Monica struggled to regain control and set things back on course. This was not in her plan, she kept telling herself. Not in her plan at all.

"MY SISTER ADDIE—SHE'S SEVEN—SAYS THIS ONE SOUNDS LIKE a ghost eating potato chips."

"No. It's a dinosaur walking on pieces of Styrofoam."

Josh braked at the stop sign and listened. It was another of his futuristic music tapes. "Hey, I think you're right." He smiled and took a hearty swig of his fresh grapefruit juice.

Monica leaned back in the van's front seat. It was almost four-thirty, and she could feel the sunburn on her face and shoulders. Her pants were still rolled up above her knees, and her hair was a mess of tangled curls. Monica gulped a strawberry protein shake, tasting in the thick sweetness a trace of the salt that still coated her mouth and face. As she raised the paper cup to get the last creamy drop, they turned onto Bedford Drive and pulled in front of her house.

She and Josh had spent the rest of the afternoon in quiet companionship—looking at the pools, planning her paper for Groener, hiking around the cliffs. Later Monica had lain in the sun while Josh had swum. It had been a lovely afternoon, but it was just the beginning of a close friendship, Monica told herself. That was all. Nothing more.

They pulled up in front of her house, a beige ranch-style with an enormous front window. Monica tied her sweatshirt around her waist, picked up her shoes, and hopped out. Bits of sand stuck to the tops of her feet and spilled out of her cuffs.

"You go ahead," Josh told her. "I have to find those books I brought for you." He crawled into the back and began sifting through the tools and coils of rope.

Monica wandered up the driveway, her skin warm, her legs loose and tired. But when she saw who was standing by her front door, everything inside stiffened. She felt as if she had just been doused with a bucket of ice water. In the doorway stood her mother, still dressed up from her business brunch, smiling at a stylish young man who stood facing her on the porch. Warren Taylor.

"There she is," said Mrs. Miller, waving to Monica. She wore a pale scarf and uncreased linen pantsuit.

Monica ran a hand through her tangled hair and tried to smile. She saw the immediate look of disapproval on her mother's face as Mrs. Miller noticed her daughter's waiflike condition.

"What have you been doing?" her mother asked.

"I went to the beach. Remember, to do my project?"

Mrs. Miller nodded in recognition and finally smiled. "Your friend Warren dropped by to visit."

In his pleated beige slacks and argyle cotton sweater, Warren looked as if he had just stepped out of a fashion spread. His blue eyes lit up when he saw her, and he smiled as if there were some sexy secret between them.

"Hi, Monica. Did you get the message that I called?"

"Huh? Oh—yes."

"I was playing tennis with a friend down the block, so I thought I'd stop by and see you."

Monica noticed her mother observing approvingly.

"Great."

Warren touched her bare shoulder. "I had to tell you that I'm going to be in the Jack Lemmon movie too."

"You are? That's wonderful."

"I shoot the same day you do. So we'll see each other."

Monica smiled. Just then Josh appeared from behind the van, carrying two textbooks. His tee-shirt was bunched up on one side, and his curly hair was an unruly mop. When he saw Warren and Mrs. Miller he stopped.

"Hi. I'm Josh Ross," he said easily.

"Hello." Mrs. Miller's voice was slightly reserved. Monica saw her mother look at Josh's old van.

Warren took a possessive step toward Monica and draped his arm around her. He gave Josh a jealous glare. Josh shifted, clearly picking up on the unspoken message. "So, how was the beach?" Warren asked.

Monica looked at her mother, and all the good feelings from her afternoon with Josh disappeared. She was tight as a drumhead. She knew she was being asked whose side she was on: Josh's or Warren's. Monica didn't know what to do. But another glance at her mother told her she had to do something. There was a pounding in her head, and she felt the tug-o'-war inside again, as if she were being pulled apart. Finally she couldn't take it anymore.

"It wasn't like some great day in the sun," she blurted out anxiously. "The only reason I went was to work on a science project for school. Josh is just helping me make it through advanced biology. That's all."

"Sounds like a lot of fun," Warren joked sarcastically.

Josh's reaction was immediate. He proudly pushed his shoulders back. His jaw became tense and his eyes angry. Dropping the two books on the porch, he said coldly, "Here are those books. See you at school."

Without saying good-bye, he turned stiffly and walked back to the van, closing his door with a proud bang. A moment later he was gone.

Monica felt something inside her die. There was an awful emptiness in her chest, and she wanted to run after Josh and tell him that she didn't mean it, that she wanted to take everything back. Seeing Josh hurt like that made her almost numb.

"What a rude young man," commented Mrs. Miller.

Monica nodded blankly. Her mother didn't know what had provoked Josh, so it was understandable that she could think that. Her mom put her arm around her. "Sweetheart, maybe Warren would like to go to the Lawrences' party?" She smiled and squeezed Monica's shoulder. "Nice to meet you, Warren. You both will excuse me. I have some calls to make."

"Nice to meet you, Mrs. Miller." Warren shook her hand, and she graciously disappeared into the house.

Monica looked down. She was still thinking about Josh when she felt Warren gently touch the bottom of her chin. She lifted her face. He was smiling at her, his dark eyes sparkling. "Hi," he whispered. "It's great to see you again."

Monica couldn't get herself to react. She looked at Warren and felt nothing. He seemed like a picture in a magazine, beautiful but not quite real. He moved closer and took both her hands.

"Oh, hi. Have you been here long?" she managed to reply.

He shook his head. "I just talked to your mom a little. She's really nice. Sorry to just drop by without calling ... but I really wanted to see you."

"You did?" He smelled of a wonderful, musky aftershave. Monica noticed the way his hair was cut in a perfect arc over his ear. "That's terrific that you got a part in the movie too."

"Yeah." He shrugged. "It's nothing big, but I'm

waiting to hear about a really good part in this other movie. That's what I'm really excited about."

"I won't ask you what it is; that's bad luck. I'm waiting on a big one myself." She remembered "Laurie and Me" and wondered if Steven Daniels had made a decision yet.

Warren drew her hands up and held them to his mouth. With a flirtatious smile he playfully bit her knuckle.

"So, do you want to get together next weekend, after the shoot? Go to that party your mom was talking about, or something else.... I'd sure like to see you."

Monica felt confused again when she thought about the Lawrence party, but Warren squeezed her hand, flashed a perfect white smile, and brought her back. She understood why her mother had dropped the hint about Warren and the party. He was just the kind of guy she should be seen with: great-looking, charming, sophisticated. It would hardly be the same driving up to the Lawrence mansion with Josh in his father's beat-up van.

"There's a party at George Lawrence's on Saturday night," Monica offered, "you know, the guy that produced 'The Last Stranger.' Would you like to go?"

"I'd love to." He checked his watch. "I'm having dinner with this big manager, so I guess I'd better take off." He started to back up down the drive-way. "So, we'll see each other at the shoot, then?

I'll call you during the week, see how things are going."

"Okay."

Warren stopped at his car, a shiny white Triumph. "I can't wait till next weekend."

" 'Bye."

He waved and got into the convertible.

Monica sank down onto the recently watered grass and watched Warren's car disappear. It was just how she had fantasized. Warren had dropped by to see her and now they had a date. Everything was going according to plan. She thought about Warren's cobalt blue eyes and that sexy smile. She should be ecstatic. But instead she felt empty. How could her feelings have changed so much in one day?

Monica sighed and leaned over, slapping her hand against the grass. "What do you want, Miller?" she asked in a sarcastic voice, "everything to be perfect?"

It couldn't be perfect—life never was. That's what her mother had taught her. There was always some sacrifice. Monica had made her decision, and now she would stick to it. She was doing the right thing.

✿ 11

"LET'S WATCH *Carrie*."

"Um, I think I've seen it."

"Then how about *The Omen, Part Two*?"

"But part one was so creepy."

"Well, what about *Friday the Thirteenth*?"

"Oh, no, Nad. Please. That kind of movie makes me sick."

Nadia Lawrence rolled her beautiful brown eyes. She and JT were at the Beverly Hills Video Chalet, shopping for a movie to rent for Nadia's VCR. She needed to watch a movie that would really take her mind off things. But no, JT only wanted to see sentimental comedies or mushy love stories. There was no way Nadia was going to be able to sit through a love story tonight. Horror and revenge were much more akin to her mood.

JT put a soothing hand on Nadia's arm. "Nad, don't be so upset. John Shephard *does* have a term paper due on Monday. Honest. He's in my class."

Nadia irritably flicked her long, reddish hair

behind her shoulder. "I just don't know what to think." Maybe John Shephard, the hunk boy she'd invited to her party to represent the exclusive "Hills" crowd, *did* have to stay home and write a history paper. But that still didn't explain why so many other kids had said they wouldn't be able to come. Everybody couldn't be writing term papers!

Nadia drummed her fingernails along a videotape box, making an angry metallic sound. "Half the people I asked said they couldn't come. And then when I asked why, they got all mysterious— like they weren't supposed to tell me. Something weird is definitely going on!"

"Oh, Nad, it's just a busy time at school. That's all."

Nadia pounded the shelf with her fist. "What does that have to do with it? It's not like I'm asking them over to play checkers or something. This is a major Hollywood party. Nobody turns down a party like this because they're worried about a term paper. No way."

"Lisa and Mindy are coming."

"Lisa and Mindy show up anytime someone puts out a bowl of potato chips."

"Glennie and her boyfriend are coming, aren't they?"

"I guess. But what good will that do if I can't get anybody else decent?" Nadia looked at her best friend and saw that hurt look again in JT's big puppy eyes. "I know it's not your fault, JT I don't mean to take it out on you. I just can't figure it out. You have to admit it is bizarre."

JT tugged on her long earring. "I know. It is."

Suddenly a light went on inside Nadia's head. Of course. Why hadn't she thought of it before? She held JT's shoulders and looked fiercely into her friend's sweet, round face. "I just figured it out—and it is incredibly low." She hesitated, too hurt to speak the words.

"What?"

Nadia paused dramatically. "I think somebody is trying to sabotage my party."

JT looked shocked. "No ..."

Nadia pulled JT down past a television monitor that was showing *Gone with the Wind.* They huddled into a quiet corner between a poster for *Suspicion* and another for *Gremlins.* "It has to be. Somebody found out about my father's party and decided to have another party on the same night just to make me look bad."

"What makes you think that?"

Nadia was putting it together. Why had it taken her so long to figure it out? Oooh, when she thought about how easily her opponent had duped her she felt sick.

"I know I'm right, JT. When I asked Marilyn Wells if she could come and she said no, I asked her why and she started to tell me. Then she stopped and said, 'It's a secret.'" Nadia closed her eyes at the memory of that conversation. The thought that she was being excluded from something important made her ache.

"Really?"

"Yes. Even Karen Small wouldn't tell me why she couldn't come. She just said there was some-

thing else going on. That's all she would say."
Nadia gasped as she remembered more. "And do
you know what excuse Grady gave for not coming?"

"Uh-uh."

Nadia looked up at a hanging poster for *Revenge of the Nerds*. She felt like crying. "He told
me he was going to study for finals all weekend."

"Nad, maybe he is."

"Sure. JT, that is the phoniest excuse I've ever
heard. Nobody turns down a hot party to study all
weekend."

"Do you really think that's it? Maybe it's just
because you didn't invite Kristin. . . ."

"Come on, JT. Half of Hollywood is going to be
there. He can be away from her for one night.
Term papers—finals—forget it! Someone is definitely trying to spoil my party!"

"Honest?"

"I'm sure of it. It has to be another party just to
compete with mine. And whoever's giving it doesn't
want me to find out. What else could it be?"

JT realized that Nadia might be right. She had
been hearing whisperings about some mysterious
party in media class. Maybe somebody *was* out to
intentionally hurt Nadia.

"But who do you think would do something
like that?" JT asked cautiously.

Nadia paused and bit her lip. "I don't know. But
when I find out, they are going to be very, very
sorry."

"Grady, will you promise me one thing?"

Grady parked his old white Jeep and turned to

Kristin. Brushing his dark hair away from his eyes, he slid down in the seat. "For you, Legs, anything."

Kristin smiled. "Legs" was her old Minnesota nickname. She bumped her shoulder against his. "Whatever movie we rent, do you promise you won't give away the ending?"

Grady put his arm around her and nuzzled his head along her neck. "I'll think about it."

Kristin laughed. "And do you also promise not to tell me how they do every special effect?" she added.

Grady started to laugh too. He was such a movie nut that he had a hard time controlling himself when he saw an effect or a shot that pleased him.

"You said one thing," he insisted. "That's two."

Kristin gave him a playful punch in the ribs. He pulled her in and kissed her lightly on the mouth. Arms about his neck, Kristin held him for an extra moment. She was glad to see him acting more like the old Grady again. He still hadn't heard anything about Yale and had been studying and worrying all weekend. It was Sunday night and finally she had convinced him to take a break.

"Let's go in."

They hopped out of the Jeep and went into the Video Chalet, which was just off Rodeo Drive, between an art gallery and a gourmet food store. As soon as they walked in, Kristin felt her stomach clench. Even from the back view there was no mistaking the slender girl in the short leather skirt. Kristin would have known Nadia's long red hair anywhere.

Grady immediately headed for the first shelf and occupied himself sorting through the assortment of rental tapes. But Kristin knew that Nadia had spotted them. Trying to ignore her, Kristin took a video box off the shelf and started reading with great concentration. Ever since she'd started Sunset High, Nadia had been snobbish and nasty to her. Even though she'd learned to hold her own with Nadia, Kristin preferred to avoid a confrontation. She took Grady's arm and stayed behind the shelf, hoping that Nadia would just go away.

No such luck. Kristin heard the determined click of high-heeled sandals get closer and closer. When she looked up, Nadia was standing right next to them, arms folded over her low-cut jersey tank top. JT stood meekly behind her.

"Well, hello there," Nadia oozed, running the back of her hand lightly along Grady's bare arm.

He looked up, startled. "Nadia. Hi. How ya doin'?"

She smiled seductively, totally ignoring Kristin. "Great."

Grady nodded and pulled down another videotape. "Hi, JT."

"Hi." JT's voice was soft, but she did include Kristin in her greeting.

Nadia shifted her terrific body so her back was to Kristin. "Grady, you know they have those old Hitchcock movies here. You should get one. My father says the directing is amazing."

Grady shrugged in a noncommittal way. "I'm so burned-out from studying all weekend I think I just want to see one of the *Star Wars* movies. That okay with you, Legs?"

Before Kristin could answer, Nadia burst in. "Oh, Grady," she teased sexily, "I don't believe you were studying *all* weekend ... and all next weekend too? You know what they say about all work and no play." Nadia's voice was playful, but there was a serious edge underneath.

"Finals are real soon, Nad."

Nadia composed her lovely features into an imitation of innocence. "Grady, can I ask you something important?" She said it as if he were the only person capable of solving her problem.

Responding to her urgent tone, Grady put down his videotape.

"What?"

Nadia looked back at JT. "I know you told me you couldn't come to my party next weekend because you had to study. Kristin," Nadia interjected, turning toward her, "I'm sorry I didn't invite you, but it's my father's party, so I'm only allowed to invite a few people. Since a lot of movie people are going to be there, I thought it would be good for Grady to come. I'm sure you understand."

Kristin just looked at her. Since she knew that Nadia never did anything without a motive, she was trying to figure out what was behind this little scene.

"Anyway," Nadia continued, "I just wondered if maybe you really weren't coming because you had another party to go to." Nadia gave Grady a sugary smile. "I just want to know if there's some other big party the same night. Maybe I should invite kids to my father's next party or have one of my own. I just wouldn't want to spoil it for somebody else who was planning a huge bash. I'd hate that."

Kristin almost dropped her video box on the floor. What was Nadia doing? Had she found out about Grady's party? Was she going to maliciously spoil the surprise?

Grady just looked confused. "Sorry, Nad," he replied moodily. "I don't know what you're talking about. I really am just going to study."

Nadia didn't look convinced. "I think there might be another party on Saturday night. Have you heard anything—"

"Oh, I'm sure there isn't," Kristin interrupted, her pulse racing. Obviously Nadia was not sure about Grady's birthday party, but she must have heard rumors. Kristin had to change the course of the conversation before Nadia gave everything away. Wildly, Kristin picked up the first videotape within reach and stepped forward. "Grady, maybe we should watch this tonight," she said loudly. "I've heard it's really good."

Grady stared at her like she had lost her mind. Even Nadia looked a little shocked. Kristin looked down at the tape and stifled a laugh. It was a movie called *Igor, the Barbarian King*. The picture on the front featured a muscle-bound man in an animal skin carrying a lushly built woman back to his cave. Kristin blushed and started to giggle nervously.

"Gee, Legs," joked Grady, "you never told me

you went for that caveman stuff. I learn something new about you every day."

Nadia shook her head and took a step back. "I guess that kind of thing must be popular in Minnesota."

Kristin smiled blithely. "Yes. They're just beyond the Stone Age there anyway."

Grady and JT laughed. Nadia shot Kristin a disgusted look. She started to walk away, but turned back. "You're sure there's no other party on Saturday night?"

"Oh, yes," Kristin jumped in. She knew she was not a very good liar and prayed that Nadia believed her. "I'm positive."

Nadia glared. "All right. I guess I'll just go ahead with my party." She gave Grady a stunning smile and put her hand on her hip. "Grady, if you change your mind, you're still welcome. Everybody is going to be there. 'Bye."

" 'Bye."

Kristin watched Nadia and JT go up to the counter and take out a tape. She continued watching them nervously until they'd climbed into Nadia's red Mercedes, parked just out front, and finally drove away.

Grady, who'd been searching the shelves, turned to her and took *Igor, the Barbarian King* out of her hands. He had a very silly smile. "Legs, do you really want to watch this?"

"I guess I can live without it. *Star Wars* will be fine."

Putting the tape back on the shelf, he took her

hand. "I bet you'd look great swinging on one of those vines in a leopard skin."

"Yeah?" She lunged toward him and grabbed him around his waist. "But I might be the one to carry *you* back to my cave," she challenged.

"Okay with me."

Kristin leaned her head on Grady's shoulder and laughed with relief. As far as she could tell, he hadn't picked up on anything.

❁ 12

"... THEN DURING LUNCH YESTERDAY EDDIE STARTED TO ask me about what records he should bring for the party."

Kristin gripped the steering wheel as she chattered to Monica. They were driving along the Ventura Freeway, heading to the location for the movie shoot.

"Grady was standing right next to me, and the second he'd said it, Eddie realized what he'd done and made this crazy face. So then he said it was for this rhumba contest for senior week. If Grady wasn't so out of it, he'd have figured out about this party ten times by now."

A box of Winchell's doughnuts sat between them, and Kristin fished blindly, ending up with a half-eaten cruller. "Are you still sure you can't come tomorrow night?" she asked.

Monica pulled her legs up under her and tried to sound tactful. It wasn't easy when she was as excited as she was. This morning she was tensed like a compressed spring, and yet she was happy, filled with anticipation. Just thinking about the day ahead made her insides race. Matters like Grady's party seemed so faraway and trivial compared to today's shoot. It wasn't often anymore that she got a chance to act, and she wanted to treasure every wonderful minute.

"I'm sorry, Kristin. I can't," Monica said. "I really do have to go to that party at the Lawrences'." There was a pause.

"Do they always make you get up this early when they shoot movies?" Kristin asked, trying to change the subject. They were due on location at six-thirty.

"Usually. It took me forever to fall asleep last night, too. I kept going over my lines." Monica turned around to inspect the hangers full of clothes that hung in the back seat. Both girls had been instructed by the movie's wardrobe lady to bring several outfits to choose from for the shooting. "I was so excited this morning I think I woke up at four."

Monica started to turn back around when Kristin grabbed her arm.

"Wait. Don't move. The turnoff is coming up." Kristin's tone was urgent. "This is where I get off. Am I clear?"

"Wait for this car. Okay ... Go!"

Clenching her teeth, Kristin steered the old station wagon into the right-hand lane and down the off-ramp. As soon as she was off the freeway, she sank back in her seat. "Made it," she sighed.

Monica applauded as they crossed busy Ventura Boulevard and headed up into the hills. Passing a square outdoor shopping center, they drove into the heavily wooded residential area of Tarzana—named after the actor who had played Tarzan. The houses were all sprawling ranch-styles surrounded by lush tropical landscaping.

"Even if we did have to get up two hours earlier than usual, it's great to be out of school," Kristin admitted.

"I know. I'm missing a pop quiz in English." Monica opened her script and started reading over her lines.

"Monica . . ." Kristin hesitated.

Monica looked up. "Hmm?"

"Whatever happened with the biology project Josh helped you with?"

At the mention of Josh's name, Monica's high spirits sank a little. "Oh, not much," she said in a controlled voice. "I turned the paper in yesterday. I guess Groener will go for it. I have to give Josh back his books." They stopped at a light, and Monica felt Kristin staring at her. "He's sort of been avoiding me," she added.

Monica tried to get her mind back on the script, but she kept envisioning Joshua's intelligent face, his strong tan arms, the graceful way he moved. But since the day at the beach, he wouldn't even speak to her. Yesterday there had been another impromptu Frisbee game, and Monica had joined, hoping to talk to him. As soon as Josh had seen her, he had put on his Walkman and strode away. It was clear that he wanted nothing to do with her anymore.

"Why is he avoiding you?" Kristin asked pointedly.

Monica wrapped her arms around her chest. Her eyes narrowed, and her mouth became a straight line. "I don't know," she said defensively. "Anyway, you don't have to worry about me hurting him or anything, since it's pretty obvious that he doesn't like me anymore."

"Why? Did something happen at the beach?"

Monica didn't answer. She knew that Kristin wouldn't understand. How could *anyone* who hadn't grown up in Hollywood understand what she was going through? "It's no big deal," Monica reasoned. "There wasn't anything between us before, and there still isn't. Believe me. Warren is more than enough to think about."

Kristin said nothing, but her green eyes and pale, freckled face no longer looked innocent. There was a knowingness now that made Monica uncomfortable. Taking out her home-made map, Monica changed the subject. "We're almost there. Just up this hill."

Both girls peered around expectantly as they pulled onto a cul-de-sac and saw the wall of trailers lining the suburban street. A large truck filled with electrical equipment was parked near the corner, and a man was rolling a set of lights up the sidewalk. Kristin swung the car around and parked about half a block away. Two other young actors were walking up the hill, carrying clothes and talking excitedly.

Monica watched them. "I wonder if Warren is here yet," she said, trying to shake off her sudden bad mood. "He called me last night. He's got all these great auditions coming up. You know, it's so good to talk to him, because he's going through some of the same stuff I am. He really understands."

Kristin nodded.

"He's so sophisticated too."

Kristin just smiled as she got out of the car.

"Don't you think he's gorgeous?"

Kristin didn't answer for a moment.

"Kristin, don't you think he's incredibly handsome?" Monica repeated almost desperately over the hood of the car.

"Yes," Kristin admitted finally. "I think he's really handsome."

"He is," Monica told herself. "Isn't he?"

They stood in the backyard of the Tarzana home. The movie crew had covered the wooden deck with lights, cameras, sound equipment, and what looked like miles of electrical cable. Some of the crew were running about frantically, while others chattered by the pool, sipped coffee, or lazily admired the spectacular valley view.

An official-looking young woman approached Monica and Kristin. "Monica Miller?"

"Yes."

The woman whipped a walkie-talkie from her belt and spoke into it. "Miller is here," she announced, pausing for a fuzzy reply. Putting away her instrument, she looked up. "Yours is the last trailer. They want you in makeup right away."

Monica listened attentively. She loved being back on a shoot. "This is Kristin Sullivan." She gestured toward Kristin, making sure that her friend did not get ignored.

"Are you an extra?" the woman asked.

"I think I'm dancing in one of the scenes."

"You're an extra," the woman corrected her. "You can wait in the living room. You won't need any makeup for the first few shots. We'll call you when we need you." The woman rushed off toward the house.

"She's one of the assistant directors," Monica explained as they walked toward the trailers. "She kind of organizes things." They walked a little further. Immediately outside the house were two large motor homes. "Those are the stars' dressing rooms," Monica said, her voice tinged with excitement.

Kristin stood on her tiptoes and tried to look in. The curtains were closed. "Jack Lemmon?" she gasped.

"Where!" Monica cried, throwing aside her professional demeanor.

Kristin made a face. "Nowhere. It just says his name on the door."

Both girls laughed. "Well, then he's inside. Who's in the other one?"

Kristin moved to the next trailer. "Jacqueline Bisset," she whispered gleefully.

When they reached the end of the row, they found Monica's trailer, which she shared with several other actresses who had speaking parts. The trailer was divided into different compartments, each about the size of a train sleeper—

just big enough to hang clothes, wash up, or sit and relax in.

"I guess I have to go right to makeup." Monica hung up her extra clothes and quickly backed out. As they started back toward the house, they were intercepted by Warren.

"Monica," he called, "I've been looking for you." He wore an off-white sportscoat and dark slacks. Aviator sunglasses dangled from one hand. Kristin could imagine him as the young love interest on "Dynasty."

"Did you just get here?" he asked, tugging at one of his shirt cuffs.

"Yes. Did you hear anything about that other movie audition?" Monica asked.

Warren winked and squeezed her shoulder. "Nothing positive yet, but it looks really good. How about you?"

"You mean 'Laurie and Me'? Nothing yet." She held up two crossed fingers, and he grabbed them, bringing her hand to his mouth for a quick kiss. Monica blushed furiously, but she seemed pleased by his attentions. As soon as they reentered the house, Monica's professionalism took over. She waved good-bye to Warren and Kristin, then headed into the kitchen, where the makeup man had set up shop.

Warren smiled quickly at Kristin. "She's great," he said, smoothing back his dark hair.

Kristin nodded—she didn't know what else to say—and together they headed for the sunken living room, which had been set up for the extras. About fifteen kids lounged on the couches, eating rolls from a large paper box and drinking coffee. It reminded Kristin of the casting office—the same gossip and primping, plus a restless, hopeful kind of feeling. She and Warren sat down together in a couple of canvas-backed chairs.

They stayed there for quite a while. Kristin contented herself with watching all that was going on—prop people rushing in and out, assistant directors calling on their walkie-talkies, the hair stylist wandering around in an apron covered with clips and bobby pins. Finally the extras were called outside, where an assistant director arranged them on the back porch. Kristin could see Monica—now in punk attire—off toward the house. She was standing with Jack Lemmon, surrounded by lights, cameras, and scores of crew members. Even from across the deck she could admire her friend's competent gestures and sureness. Clearly Monica was in her element.

The scene they were shooting involved a father coming home unexpectedly and finding a teenage party. While he confronted his daughter, Monica, Kristin and the other extras would be just visible in the background, dancing and cavorting. An assistant director named John Pepper waved his hands, and the extras gathered for his instructions.

"Okay, kids, all you extras," he began in a slight Italian accent, hands cupped over his mouth. He was an energetic young man in shorts and a sweatshirt. "When you hear 'action,' I want you to party it up. Dance, move around. Nothing big or noisy, just background activity. Anybody dancing, watch me for the beat. We'll put the music in

later, but I want you all moving to the same song.
Make it look like you're having a good time. Got
it?"

The group nodded a collective yes and ambled
into position. Feeling unsure, Kristin sidled over
to Warren, the only familiar face. But he didn't
notice her. He was talking to a stunning blonde in
a low-cut jumpsuit.

"So maybe you and I should be a couple neck-
ing in the back," Kristin heard him say to the
actress. The blonde smiled dumbly and giggled.
Warren moved in closer and gave the blonde a
sexy wink.

Kristin couldn't help but think that he was carrying his part too far. Warren didn't need to sug-
gest that. If he really liked Monica, why was he
making a pass at someone else? But her thoughts
were interrupted when the assistant director called
for quiet.

"Action!"

Suddenly the group bubbled into a party. A
goofy redheaded boy grabbed Kristin's hand and
started to dance with her. Two couples over to
the side were doubled over in silent laughter. As
Kristin spun around, her eyes bugged open as she
caught a glimpse of Warren. He and the blonde
were entwined in a romantic lip-lock.

But as soon as John Pepper called "Cut!" the
feverish activity stopped. The couple stopped
laughing, the redheaded boy released her hand,
Warren let go of the fluffy blonde. Kristin leaned
back against a beam to rest, wishing with all her
heart that she could just stop thinking for a little

while. Even though she didn't know much about acting, she didn't like the way the scene was shaping up.

"How do you like that, doll? No more freckles!" The middle-aged makeup man was covering Kristin's pale skin with peachy pancake makeup.

"It's the tan I'll never have," Kristin bantered back. She closed her eyes as he smoothed the damp sponge over every corner of her face. They'd gotten through the morning scenes, but there was work left to do. Still full from the huge catered lunch, Kristin sat at the kitchen table, getting ready for a later scene in which she might have a close-up.

"Doll," the chubby fellow gestured wildly, "I'm afraid you'll have to unbutton your three top buttons and let me do your neck. Otherwise you'll look like Frankenstein's monster." He leaned in and whispered, "Don't worry. The boys can't come over here. Those beasts."

Kristin laughed and unbuttoned. The kitchen had been divided into a boys' and a girls' section with a makeshift curtain. The makeup man modestly stuck tissues in the neckline of her blouse before coating the pancake down past her collarbone. Then he handed her a wand of mascara. "It's easier if you just do this yourself, doll."

"Okay." Kristin leaned into the lighted mirror as the makeup man rushed out to powder down Jackie Bisset. She had started to brush on the mascara when she overheard a conversation from the boys' side of the curtain. When she recognized Warren's voice, she put down the brush and listened intently.

"Oh, man," she heard Warren moan, "I had to bust my buns to get this crummy day as an extra."

"Me too," answered another actor.

"If I don't get a good agent soon, I swear I'm going to go nuts." Warren's voice again.

"Yeah, but what do you do?" piped up the other guy. "You can't get a part without an agent, and no agent wants to talk to you unless you've already had a part."

"I know. That's all I've heard for a year now. But I may be about to get a break. I just met Rosalind Miller."

"Are you kidding?" The other actor sounded very impressed. "Wow, Roz Miller is really big. How did you get in to see her?"

"That's a trade secret. But if I play things right, I just might get her to represent me."

"Seriously?"

"She already invited me to a party at George Lawrence's. Half the big people in this town are going to be there...." The voices trailed off as the boys left by the side door.

Kristin let the mascara fall in her lap as she leaned her head into her hands. She was so shocked that she just sat there, unable to budge. What was going on? Warren had told her that he had tons of agents interested in his career. He had told Monica that he was up for a big movie part! And yet from what Kristin had just heard, it sounded as if he was desperate ... as if he was having no luck at all with his career. Was his interest in Monica for only one reason—to get to her mother? How could anyone do that! How could he lead Monica on when all he wanted was to use her?

"What a jerk," Kristin whispered furiously. One thing was for sure, though. If Warren was just out to use Monica, he wasn't going to get away with it. Not as long as she was around.

When it came time to film her second scene, Kristin had difficulty concentrating. All she could think about was Warren and the way he was using Monica. She and three other extras stood out on the patio and received instructions from Stephen Book, the director.

Book was no longer the playful fellow that Kristin had met at the audition. He now looked tired and impatient and kept pulling on his beard with nervous strokes. He called Kristin over with an impatient wave.

"You," he ordered gruffly, "start here." Kristin looked down. "Here" referred to a spot on the patio marked with an X in silver tape.

"And walk slowly over to there," Book continued, pointing to where another crew member had stuck another silver X to the floor. "Then stop and smile and go off camera toward the pool. Understand?"

Kristin nodded. It didn't seem too hard.

"Okay," Book ordered. "Let's do it."

A chubby woman rushed in front of Kristin with

a tiny blackboard and clapped down the wooden
stick attached to the top. Having announced the
take and scene, she scrambled off and the cameras moved in.

"Action!"

Kristin started to walk. But on her second step
her foot caught on a piece of electrical cable and
she clumsily lurched forward.

"Cut!"

Kristin looked around guiltily.

"Try not to break your leg and do it again," the
director ordered, his hand rubbing his temple.

Kristin took a deep breath. She had had no idea
it would be so hard. She tried it once more. But
this time she looked down at the floor to make
sure she was on her mark, the silver X.

"Don't look down. Do it again! And smile this
time."

Kristin was starting to sweat. Backing up to her
starting point—the whole move was no more than
five feet—she was beginning to have great re-
spect for Monica's craft. This time she memorized
the exact number of steps she would take and
started again.

"Action!"

Three more takes and Kristin finally got it right.
She didn't look down or forget to smile. Stepping
out of the range of the camera, she raised her
arms over her head in glee and relief. Then she
heard a crash and felt herself jolt forward. She
had just walked right into a lighting fixture.

"Oh, no. I'm sorry," she yelped immediately.

"It's okay. We've got the shot," reassured an

elderly crewman who helped her up. "You're done. No damage."

Kristin smiled weakly and retreated into the house. How Monica ever did all that and spoke lines at the same time was beyond her comprehension.

Monica still had one more scene to shoot, and Kristin looked for a quiet place to recover and wait. On her way to the living room she passed a small, book-lined study. Inside was Warren, all alone, relaxing in an easy chair and flipping through a magazine.

Kristin's mind immediately clicked with a plan. Before she squealed to Monica she had to make sure that her suspicions were correct. She had to find out just what Warren was made of. Impulsively, she stepped into the study and closed the door behind her.

"Hi."

Warren looked up lazily, gave her an indifferent smile, and went back to his issue of *Us*.

Kristin slipped down onto the sofa. She wasn't sure exactly what she was going to do until she did it. With a glance toward Warren, she picked up the telephone from the end table between them. Warren was still engrossed in an article titled "The Hottest Young Actors in Hollywood."

Kristin punched her home phone number. But just before the ringing started she pressed on the cradle, breaking the connection.

"Hello?" She was answered by a dial tone. "This is Kristin. Can I talk to my father?" She turned her back to Warren, sure that if he saw her face he'd know she was bluffing. Just this once she wished she were a better liar. Deciding she had waited long enough for her "father" to come to the phone, she spoke again.

"Hi, Daddy." She made a face. She never called her father "Daddy." Still, Warren didn't know her well enough to realize how unnatural she sounded.

"Yes, we finished shooting. It went fine." She took a deep breath and forged ahead. "There are a few guys working as extras here that might be able to play that part on your new TV show."

Kristin glanced over at Warren from the corner of her eye. Sure enough, he had just put down his article. His interest had shifted to her.

"Do you want me to get any names for you? Oh, I see, just tell them to call your office. Okay. I will. I'll be home pretty soon. See you then. 'Bye." Kristin set down the phone and started to leave. Warren's voice stopped her.

"Kristin, don't go." He was looking at her longingly. "Boy, was I hoping you'd come in here."

"You were?"

He stood up and gently took her hand, coyly caressing her fingers. Slowly he brought her pinky up to his mouth and kissed it. "All day I've been trying to figure out a way to talk to you alone. It's been driving me crazy." His voice was oozing with seduction. He slid down onto the sofa, easily pulling her with him. Kristin was mesmerized by him. Warren was a lot different from the boys she was used to. His moves were practiced and skillful. He looked her up and down with his dark, sexy eyes.

But Kristin didn't find those eyes sexy anymore. Suddenly they looked as empty as little glass marbles. She wondered why she hadn't seen right off that he was a phony. But before she knew it, his arm had wound itself around the back of her neck. He moved closer.

"You are really beautiful," he said with his best actor's sincerity.

"Thank you." Kristin was disgusted at how swiftly he had taken her bait. As he ran his hand up the back of her neck and through her long hair, Kristin felt oddly detached —as if this were happening to someone else. It was like a movie scene and she was watching from the outside. Part of her was disgusted, but part of her was fascinated to see how far Warren thought he could go.

Warren grimaced. "I don't know how it happened. I was attracted to you all along, but somehow Monica thought I liked her. I didn't want to hurt her, and I knew you had a boyfriend." Warren's arm had wound itself around her back. He pulled her to him. "But I just can't get you off my mind."

Kristin knew things had gone far enough when she felt Warren lean in to kiss her. She hardly needed any more proof and raised her hand to push him away. But Warren caught her arm playfully and pulled her even closer. Kristin turned her face away and was just about to tell him off when she heard the door open. The wooden bang was followed by a violent gasp. Kristin froze. Her heart stopped when she saw who was standing in the doorway....

Monica.

Warren jumped up and Kristin fell onto the carpet. Her mind reeled as she desperately tried to collect her wits. But when she looked at Monica's face, her breath caught in her throat. Standing before them in a huge white tee-shirt and tight punk jeans, Monica looked like a kid who had just awakened from a nightmare—her short hair slicked back, her big eyes like two open wounds. Kristin scrambled to her feet. She started to speak, to explain ... to justify what Monica had just seen.

But it was too late. Monica was already gone.

✽ 13

"MONICA, YOU DON'T BELIEVE ME. . . ."

Monica sat very still and silent, but her fists were tight little balls, and she was turned away from Kristin, her shoulders hunched over protectively. She almost couldn't contain the storm inside her—feelings of rage and betrayal, surprise, embarrassment, and self-doubt. This was her reward, she told herself, for opening up, for trusting someone when she should have known better. Well, never again. Her mother was right. The most important thing was her career—that was all you could count on. Friends and boyfriends would only disappoint her. Just look at her own father.

"Monica, listen to me," Kristin pleaded, slowing the car to a crawl. The afternoon traffic was backed up—probably an accident up ahead. She anxiously flicked back her long light-brown hair and glanced over. Her pale skin was still coated with orangy makeup, and mascara was smudged under her green eyes.

"Monica, I'm telling you, he just wants to use

you to get to your mother. That's why he made a pass at me, because he thought my father ..."

Monica brought her hands to her ears and refused to listen. She could still see Kristin and Warren entwined on the sofa, practically on top of each other. She cringed as she remembered opening the door. It felt like a blow, a slap. And now Kristin expected her to believe some ridiculous story about her father? The midwesterner had gotten one glimpse of the Hollywood scene and had become as hungry as every other aspiring starlet. "It's bad enough you used me to get a job on this movie," she said bitterly.

"I don't care about being in the movies," Kristin burst out. "This was just a fluke. Monica, come on. I don't care if I never step on a movie set again."

"Oh, sure," Monica countered. "You wanted to be in the movie and then you decided to move in on Warren. I was a perfect way for you to get everything."

Both girls suddenly lurched forward as Kristin hit the brakes, almost plowing into the car in front. She pounded her palm against the old dashboard and furiously faced Monica. "You really have a problem, you know that! You have absolutely no idea who's a real friend and who isn't!"

"All I know is that a real friend wouldn't have thrown herself at my boyfriend."

"I didn't. I think Warren is a creep! How can you even care about him?"

"You obviously do...."

"Listen to me!" Kristin ranted. "You have a real

problem. You ignore Josh except when you want to use him, and then you won't believe it when this jerk tries to use *you!*"

Monica's head was pounding. She couldn't respond.

"I don't think you'd know the difference between a real friend and a phony if they had signs on their chests. And you know why?"

"Why?"

"Because lately all you think about is using people, so you assume that's what everybody else is doing to you. Except for the one person who really is, then you think the jerk's perfect. I don't understand you at all. It's sad."

"Don't worry about me. I know what I saw!" Monica looked out the window as they slowly passed the scene of the accident. A sports car was totally smashed on one side and a young man was holding a cloth to his forehead. They passed by and the traffic speeded up.

Monica switched on the radio. Anything to keep from talking to Kristin. A radio talk show came on featuring the soothing female voice of a popular call-in psychologist. The caller was young. Monica slunk down in the seat and listened.

"Dr. King?" the girlish voice questioned.

"Go on," the doctor soothed.

"So anyway, my mom won't even talk to Jed, my boyfriend, because he just works in a grocery store. I don't know who she expects me to be with, Prince Charles or something. But she says she doesn't even want to talk to me until I break up with him. And she insults him and stuff. What should I do?"

"How old are you, Amanda?" Dr. King asked.

"Nineteen."

"You know, Amanda"—Dr. King sounded so calm and sensible—"at a certain point you must stop worrying what your mother thinks. And you must trust yourself enough to establish your own values. When one is a child ..."

Abruptly Monica switched off the radio. She didn't want to hear any more. She glanced at Kristin, who was still poised over the steering column, her face tense and hurt. Monica turned to the window and looked out at the oppressive afternoon smog. Her chest was so tight it hurt. She bit the inside of her cheek and used all her energy to hold back the tears.

When Kristin got home an hour later, her house was empty. Her parents and her brother, Shawn, had already left for Santa Barbara. Greeting her was a long note from her dad, a letter from Amy, two carefully wrapped homemade dinners, and a bag of popcorn meant especially for TV-watching with Monica. But of course Monica was not sleeping over. There had been no question of that. Kristin wondered if she and Monica would ever even speak again.

Feeling hot and tired and shaky, Kristin padded into the living room and plopped down on the corduroy-covered sofa. After weeks of moving crates and bed sheets for curtains, the living room was finally furnished with the antiques from her old house. The maple rocker, with the carved spokes, the old coal box that they used as an end table, the glass china cabinet filled with her mother's beloved collection of antique plates—they all fit in the modern room, and yet looked slightly out of place.

"Just like me," Kristin grumbled.

She felt that way again. Like a stranger in a strange land. She kicked off her jogging shoes, put her feet up on the maple coffee table. Monica was the first friend she had made at Sunset High. It was Monica who had seen her through the bumpy beginnings with Grady and the difficult adjustment to her new environment. When Kristin had been so upset that all she wanted was to hide from the world, Monica had been the one to help her snap out of it. Now it was Monica who was hiding, crumbling under the pressures of life in Beverly Hills. And Kristin had tried to show her the truth, but it had backfired. Maybe she had done it in the wrong way, though. Instead of helping, she had only succeeded in ruining their friendship.

Listlessly Kristin picked up an envelope from the coffee table and opened it. It was from Amy, her best friend back in Minnesota. The short message was bordered with Amy's famous octopus cartoons.

Dear K:

I'm sorry it's taken me so long to write back, but I've been incredibly busy doing this big article on girls' athletics for the paper. Looks like the Ontario High Axmen—or rather the "Axwomen," as we have started calling

ourselves—are going all-city in softball, swim-
ming, and gymnastics. I thought you'd want
to know. Christine and Kim are doubling as
cheerleaders and as competitors on the gym-
nastics team. Both are doing great (I think
Christine may get first in floor exercise). I'll
send you the article when it's done. Sounds
like things are going really well for you there
now. Have to go, love from everybody, miss
you.
Amy

Kristin let the short letter float to the carpet. At first Amy's letters from St. Cloud had been frequent and long, with notes from everyone in her old crowd. But life was going on without her, a new cheerleader had taken her place, and by now no one probably noticed the difference. Kristin was caught in the middle. No longer a small-town girl from St. Cloud, she was still far from understanding the ways of Hollywood.

She felt empty and alone. More than anything she wanted to call Grady, to be with him. He was the one person who bridged the gap. He was one hundred percent Beverly Hills, but accepted and appreciated who she really was. Kristin glanced at the phone.

Quickly she pulled the sofa's needlepoint pillow in to her chest and hugged.

No! She couldn't call him. The arrangement was to ignore Grady all weekend ... so that the surprise would be that much more startling. Besides, in her current mood she would probably blab uncontrollably, giving away the secret. She would have to wait until tomorrow and somehow survive the night in this strange, empty house by herself. Kristin was just getting ready to go upstairs when the phone rang.

"Hello."

"Hi, Kristin, it's Josh."

It was good to hear a friendly voice. "Hi."

"You okay?" he asked immediately. "You sound sort of weird."

Kristin hesitated. Of course sensitive Josh would pick up on her distress. She decided not to burden him with it. She knew that his feelings for Monica were complicated enough.

"I'm all right. It's just been a long day, shooting that movie and all."

"How'd it go?"

"It was hard. I have a feeling I'm not destined to be a movie star."

Josh laughed. "There are worse things." His voice became more serious. "Listen, I called because we have a problem with the party."

"Oh, no. What?"

"Two of my little brothers just came down with raging measles. They're really sick. I don't think we should have the party here. Can you think of any place where we could have it instead?"

Kristin's shoulders slumped forward in disappointment. How could they find another location for the party in one day? After all their planning, she couldn't bear the thought of canceling it.

"What about your house?" suggested Josh. "I could call everybody and make sure they all know."

Kristin looked around the antique-filled living room. It was a good idea, but what about her parents? She could call them later tonight and ask ... but if she did, there was the possibility—the distinct possibility—that they would say no. Then what would they do? There would be no time for an alternate plan. Her parents weren't coming back until Sunday afternoon. Surely they could remove all traces by then. Grady's friends were all responsible and considerate.

Josh broke into her thoughts. "I'll help you set up tomorrow. If you want, I'll come over on Sunday too, and help you clean up afterward. I feel bad to spring this on you at the last minute, but I don't know what else to do."

"It's not your fault." Kristin hesitated a moment longer, looking around the room. She took a deep breath. "Okay, let's have the party over here."

"Great."

Kristin told herself that nothing could possibly go wrong. Or could it?

Spread out on her low bed, Monica lay with her face buried in a pillow. More than anything she wanted this awful tugging feeling to stop. She wanted to know which way was the right way. She wanted to know what she should do.

The phone rang and she was relieved for the distraction. She prayed that it was Warren. Somehow he'd make it all better. Monica picked up the phone at the same time as her mother who was working in the study. As soon as she heard Warren's voice she felt some of her tightness ease. He was calling to explain. He would tell her something that would prove that it was all Kristin's fault. Warren would set her world straight again.

"Hold on, Warren. I'll get Monica," her mother said in a preoccupied tone. Monica could see her, glasses on, script before her. All business.

Monica was just about to say hello when Warren interrupted urgently. "Mrs. Miller, wait. Uh, actually I called to talk to you." His sugar-coated tone sent a jolt through Monica.

"Uh, Monica and I had a sort of falling-out, but I still want to talk to you about my career. You know, what we were discussing the other day when I dropped by ... that maybe I could come in to your office and talk to you about representing me." He was speaking quickly, as if he were afraid she'd hang up on him.

"I think I'm really going to have a big career if I can just find the right people to help me. You know Gail Morrison, at Warner Brothers; she had me in to read, and she thinks I'm going to to be very hot; maybe you could—"

Mrs. Miller cut him off. "Warren, why don't you call me at the office on Monday? Maybe I can set up a meeting with one of my assistants."

"Really? Oh, that would be great. Thank you, Mrs. Miller. I really appreciate ..."

"I'm not promising anything. Just call my secretary on Monday, and we'll see what we can do."

"Great. I'll do that. Thank you, Mrs. Miller."

"Did you want to talk to Monica?"

Warren laughed uncomfortably. "That's okay. I'll talk to her later. Thanks."

"Good-bye, Warren."

Monica let her hand go limp and dropped the receiver. She felt all the energy drain out of her body. She felt sick. Kristin had been right. Monica had heard Warren's voice, oozing with concern for only one thing—his career. She had been used. How could she have ever believed he cared about her? He didn't care about anything except himself.

She crumpled up on her bed. Amid the white pillows and high-tech furniture she spotted one incongruous object—a small stuffed dog, yellow and mangy, left over from her childhood. The dog was one thing she'd never been able to give away. Monica wrapped it in her arms. It smelled dusty and safe.

How could she have been so blind? Was she so concerned with her own career that she didn't know a true friend from a false one? Maybe she was just as bad as Warren. Down deep she'd known that Kristin would never deceive her, but something had gotten crossed inside that had made her feel as if she had to side with Warren. It didn't matter how she'd really felt. Just as it didn't matter how she felt about whatever she was required to do to further her acting career.

There was a soft knock at the door, and Monica looked up. The door opened tentatively and her mother walked in. "You're awake."

Monica sat up. She had pretended to be napping since her mother had gotten home from work.

"Your friend Warren just called." Mrs. Miller sat next to her on the platform bed. Her glasses were pushed up like a headband, and she wore a long nylon robe over a pair of lounging pajamas. Without makeup she always looked older and more tired.

"He's not my friend anymore."

"He told me that you two had a disagreement. Are you upset?"

Monica turned away, hugging the dog even harder.

Her mother looked at her affectionately. "Monica, Warren asked me to help him. He's probably got a future in the business. If you want me to introduce him to some people, I will. Would you like me to?"

Monica could not look her mother in the eye.

Her mother prompted her. "Honey, would you like me to help Warren?"

Monica took a short, sharp breath. "Mom, the only reason he was paying attention to me at all was to get to you."

Mrs. Miller sighed and touched Monica's back. "So that's it. I wondered what was going on." She tipped Monica's chin and made her look up. "Honey, I'm sorry he hurt your feelings, but it's not such a crime. It's difficult to get started, and Warren obviously wants it very badly. You can't blame him too much."

Suddenly Monica felt a huge swell of anger. All the rage that she had been holding back was about to bubble over. "How can you say that? He really hurt me. He used me and you would still help him? Mom, how could you do that?"

Mrs. Miller sat ramrod-straight, her lips pinched

together. "I realize that there is no excuse for his leading you on, but you have to be more adult about these things."

"But I'm not an adult! I'm seventeen, and when somebody treats me that way it makes me feel awful. I don't care how old I get. It's always going to make me feel awful!" Her voice was getting loud and high.

Her mother put her hand to her forehead as if she had a headache. "You are being very emotional about this. But I think it's clear that I should have nothing to do with Warren professionally. I'll tell him that when he calls on Monday. All right?"

Monica was still furious. "No, it's not all right! I don't care if you help him or not. That's not what's important. What matters is that he's a creep and that you think what he did is okay!"

"Monica," Mrs. Miller said, standing up, "you're upset now. When you calm down you'll see that you're making too much out of this whole thing."

Monica slammed her hand against a pillow. Things were becoming clear to her for the first time in weeks. She was furious at her mother, at Warren, and most of all at herself. She had been trying to mold herself into everyone's vision of the perfect Monica at the expense of the flesh-and-blood one. She was tired of being what she thought everyone else wanted her to be. She had to start figuring out things on her own.

"I couldn't make too much out of this," Monica exploded. "It's too important. You think what Warren did is okay because you think that using people and hurting them just to help your career is okay. Well, I don't!"

Her mother's face was turning red. "I have told you how I feel about this. I started out all alone in this business, and I found out the hard way how things work. If you want to get slapped around ... well ... you just go ahead!"

"I don't see how it could make me feel worse than I do now. Just because my father left you and you decided that making it was the most important thing in the world doesn't mean I have to be the same way. Nothing can be that important!"

Her mother backed into the doorway. She clenched the doorknob so hard that her knuckles were white. "You have a lot to learn, Monica."

"Maybe I do. But I know I don't want to be so obsessed with my career that I don't have any friends or any other life. I did that for four years when I was little and that's enough. It's just not worth it."

Her mother glared at her. "You were lucky to have been on that show...."

"I'm tired of hearing how lucky I was or how I have to be a grownup and hurt people because I'm so lucky. That's not luck. That's horrible."

"Fine. You haven't seemed to mind all the work we've been doing to get you back on a TV show," her mother countered fiercely. "And while we're talking about this—I want you to think about what you're going to say to Mr. Daniels tomorrow night and who you're going to take. Obviously Warren is out...."

"Mom, haven't you heard me at all? I'm not going to that party tomorrow night. Not even if the entire rest of my career depends on it!"

There was an awful silence. "What did you say?"

"I'm not going to the party at the Lawrences'."

Her mother's handsome face was taut with anger. "Monica, don't be an idiot."

Monica stood up. "There's a party for Grady, Kristin Sullivan's boyfriend, and that's where I'm going instead."

Her mother was trembling, and Monica suddenly wished they could both just break down and cry. But it was out of control now, and only getting worse. Her mother pointed at her. "Do you want to have a career or not?"

"I want a career, but I'm not willing to do anything to get it."

"Great," her mother spat out. "Do what you want, Monica. Just don't come to me for help." Mrs. Miller slammed the door.

Monica burst into tears. She had finally let go of the rope; the awful tug-o'-war was over. She was exhausted from the struggle and her bruises were fresh, but she knew that if she just gave herself a chance, she would be able to get up again.

It was like after "The Twain Family" ended. She thought that she would cease to exist without the show, without being somebody important. When people stopped recognizing her, she felt as if her life were over. Gradually, though, she'd realized that there were other things—friends, school, the

Monica who *wasn't* an actress. But lately she had lost her perspective again because she was struggling so hard to climb back up. She had been willing to do anything for success. She still wanted to be an actress, and she would be. But she wouldn't use and hurt people to get there.

Monica thought about Kristin and how lucky she was to have such a loyal friend. If only she had trusted her. If only she could make Kristin trust her again.

And there was someone else that Monica couldn't get out of her mind. She had been trying all week to erase the image of his face, the sound of his voice. . . .

"Josh."

As Monica said his name the tears flowed again. Throaty sobs heaved from deep inside. For the first time she had found a boy she could open up to and communicate with. Yet she had done everything possible to cover up her attraction to him, and it had nearly torn her apart. That was what the tug-o'-war had been about, that was why her life had felt like one big wrestling match.

She had hurt Josh. Badly. But was there anything she could do now to make him forgive her? No. The damage was done. There was no going back.

Monica put her head down on the pillow and slowly closed her eyes.

❀ 14

"LET'S GO TO GUCCI'S. LIKE I NEED TO GET A BELT, okay?" said Lisa White in her drawn-out California voice.

Mindy Lockwood, the good-looking daughter of a studio executive, objected. "Wait. I want to try this on." She held up a matching denim jacket and jeans, both with exotically situated pockets and zippers. They were in MGA/ Guess, the popular boutique on Rodeo Drive.

"Maybe I'll try these on too," said JT, holding up a pair of straight-legged jeans. She pulled on her earring and looked to Nadia for approval. When her beautiful best friend shook her head no, JT hung the pants back up.

Nadia strolled slowly around the shop, just brushing the clothes with her fingertips. The store was packed with sportswear, and racks were overflowing with jeans of every cut and pastel wrinkled cottons. Chic displays and bright posters were plastered on the walls. Ordinarily Nadia would have outshopped anybody, but today she wasn't tempted. Even the loud punk music couldn't rouse her.

Instead, Nadia was bored ... and disappointed. Her plans to make her father's party the social coup of the semester had failed. Oh, kids were coming. Popular, important kids. But many of her first string list had turned her down, and she still didn't know why. The explanation that she might have already lost her social clout was unacceptable to Nadia. She knew with absolute certainty that there was more to it.

"I'm going to get a gelato," Nadia said moodily, referring to the fancy Italian ice cream that was the current rage. "Anybody else want one?"

Lisa popped her curly head over the dressing room door. She had changed her mind about leaving for Gucci's and was pulling on a cotton tank top. "No way. I didn't take class at Jane Fonda's like you did."

Mindy was now laden down with an armload of denims and shook her head. "Forget it. You might as well just plaster that stuff right on my thighs."

JT looked longingly, but, with a touch to her waistline, forced herself to abstain too.

"Okay. I'll meet you all back here." Nadia slung her Louis Vuitton bag over her shoulder and walked out onto Rodeo Drive.

It was a mild, slightly humid day. Traffic was heavy, and the sidewalks were cluttered with tourists. Nadia was cutting across the street, toward Florenza Gelato, when she saw a junky green van pull into a parking space just ahead of her. She would not have paid any attention to the trashy old vehicle had she not caught Kristin Sullivan's profile in the passenger seat. Curious, Nadia stepped into the marble entrance to the ice cream parlor and watched. Kristin hopped down from the van, wearing a sweat shirt and flowing cotton skirt. She was followed by Joshua Ross.

Nadia backed up further into the shop. She didn't know Josh well—ever since she'd discovered that his mother was the Sunset High nurse, she hadn't considered him worth getting to know. But because he was good-looking and Grady's best friend, she often found herself watching him. The trouble was, Josh gave her the impression that no matter what she did, he was not impressed. Nadia kept her eye on the pair as she sauntered over to the ice cream counterman.

"What would you like?" asked the young counterman.

At that moment, Kristin and Josh went into Let's Party, the small party shop just around the corner. Why were they going into Let's Party unless there was another event in the works? Nadia wondered, overcome with suspicion. Without a word to the young man, she spun around and headed back out to the street.

Nadia didn't have much practice at trying to look inconspicuous, but she did her best. Quietly she slipped into the small art deco shop and parked herself behind a tall aisle of greeting cards. Head down, she pretended to read card after card while straining to catch bits of Josh and Kristin's conversation.

Josh was pulling down a few rolls of crepe

paper streamers and tossing them to Kristin, who caught them with athletic ease. Nadia scooted down until she was close to them, just on the other side of the aisle. Kristin attempted to juggle and laughed as the rolls dropped onto the floor.

"You'll have to get Eddie to show you how. I've even seen him juggle bananas," Josh teased.

Kristin laughed. "Somehow that doesn't surprise me." She took down a package of balloons. "So Eddie has everything under control for tonight. He's going to get Grady to the party?"

"Grady thinks they're studying together. He's going to stop at your house, supposedly because you borrowed Eddie's library card and he has to get it back."

"I can't believe Grady's not suspicious. Tell me Eddie has ever studied on a Saturday night. Is there anybody who still doesn't know that the party's been changed to my house?"

"Just John Shephard. Nobody was home, but I'll try again later. Oh, and I left a message on Marilyn Wells's answering machine."

"I'm sure she'll get it."

As Josh and Kristin started to walk toward the register, Nadia froze, every toned muscle in her body knotted up. She had heard enough. If she hadn't wanted to keep her cover, she would have started yelling then and there. She clenched her teeth and breathed hard.

Kristin Sullivan had deliberately lied to her. The innocent-looking midwesterner *had* been planning a party all along and had concealed the information. She had underestimated Kristin, who

obviously was out to get revenge on Nadia for
making a play for Grady. Now everything was
falling into place. Kristin had just been biding her
time, waiting until she could get Nadia into a
corner where it would really hurt ... and she had
succeeded.

Nadia fought her tears and vowed to stay in the
game. What Kristin had done was cruel and sneaky.
Nadia would figure out some way to get back at
her. She didn't know what it would be, but she
wanted to make sure that Kristin Sullivan felt just
as miserable as she did.

Right after dinner, Monica put on her baggy
plaid pants, suspenders, Camp Beverly Hills sweatshirt, and plastic shoes. Without saying good-bye
to her mother she slipped on her safety helmet
and rode her Vespa motor scooter over to Kristin's
house.

The only nonmansion on Rexford Drive, the
Sullivan house was a modern two-story with a
huge oak tree and what looked like a recently
planted flower bed in front. Monica walked slowly
up the driveway, took a deep breath, and rang the
bell.

When Kristin opened up and saw her, her expression reflected curiosity, distrust, and hope.
Her long hair was haphazardly tied up, a roll of
masking tape was around her wrist, and she held
an old paintbrush. She made no move to invite
Monica in.

Monica nervously flicked her dark bangs out of
her eyes. "Hi."

Kristin just looked at her, now mostly curious.

Monica cleared her throat and hugged her helmet against her side. "Um, I came over because I wanted to talk to you about yesterday." Monica looked down. She cleared a stray leaf off the doormat with her foot. "I'm sorry. I should have believed you. You were telling the truth about Warren."

The distrust faded from Kristin's face, and the hope took over. "I'm sorry too," she said quietly. "I picked such a dumb way to prove it to you."

"It's okay. I wouldn't have believed you no matter what you did," Monica admitted. "I had to find out for myself."

Kristin paused. "I know there's some stuff I don't understand, but he wasn't worth wrecking our friendship over."

"Don't worry. You were right about Warren" —Monica's voice caught in the back of her throat— "and about me too. I'm really sorry."

"Do you want to come in and help us set up before you go to Nadia's?" Kristin offered. "We're having the party here now."

"You are?" Monica stood up straight. "Actually, I decided not to go to Nadia's father's after all." Her voice got shy and childlike. "Am I still invited to Grady's party?"

Kristin grinned. "Oh, of course." She spread her long arms, and they came together for a warm hug. For a moment the girls stood in the doorway and held each other—Kristin taller and fairer, Monica darker and more delicate. Finally, they parted, and Kristin took Monica's helmet. "Come on in."

Her arm intertwined with Kristin's, Monica followed her friend inside and heard all about the change in plans and Kristin's decision not to tell her parents and how Eddie was going to fool Grady into coming. Monica accompanied Kristin down the hall, feeling more at ease than she had in days. But when they reached the living room, she spotted a figure balanced atop an old step ladder, and her insides twisted up again.

"Hi, Josh," Monica said. Afraid to meet his eye and yet yearning to look at his strong face, Monica settled for staring at the bottom of the step ladder. She was barely aware of Kristin slipping away into the kitchen. All she knew was that she and Josh were suddenly alone.

He had been taping a "Happy Birthday" banner to the ceiling. When he saw her he stopped and relaxed on the top of the ladder. In his corduroy shirt, khaki shorts, and old running shoes, he looked rugged, and relaxed.

"Do you want some help?"

He looked up at the homemade sign. "No thanks. It's all done. What's up?" He looked down at her with a strangely removed expression and tapped the tape against his palm.

His coolness made Monica take a step back. This was the way he had been toward her all week. She had been trying to convince herself that it didn't matter, but his distance really had hurt her deeply. "I guess I'm the first guest to arrive. I'm pretty early. It's a good thing I stopped

by. I didn't know the party was changed to here."
She laughed awkwardly.

Josh didn't smile. "I thought you couldn't come."

"Oh, I was supposed to go to that party at
Nadia Lawrence's and talk to Denis Daniels's father because I'm up for this TV series that he's
doing. I was supposed to go and charm him so
he'd make sure to give me this important part,
but I decided to come here instead."

She knew she was rambling. Josh didn't look
impressed by her change of heart. He just nodded
and climbed down. Folding the ladder, he tucked
it under his arm and started to leave the living
room. Monica stopped him.

"Josh."

He halted in the doorway and turned back. His
gaze pierced her like an arrow. Just this once she
wished that he really could see everything that
was going on inside her.

After a long silence Monica spoke. "I'm sorry
about after we went to the beach. I didn't mean
that ... about you just being somebody to help
me with school...." Her voice trailed off. She
didn't know what else to say and looked to Josh
for help. But he stood unmoved, his face still cool
and composed.

Monica shrugged. "I guess that's all I wanted to
say."

They looked at each other, but Monica could
tell that her words had not had much effect.
Unlike Kristin, who was so quick to forgive and
start over, Josh remained distant and proud. He
shook his head sadly.

"I'm sorry too," he said at last; then he picked up the ladder and walked out.

Denis Daniels was restless. He paced his bedroom, did a drumroll on his dresser top with his favorite sticks, took the backs off his stereo speakers to examine the insides, read half an article in *Rolling Stone*, then started to pace again. He had to get out of the house. He was going crazy.

Crushing two silk-covered pillows into a comfortable ball, he put them under his head and stretched out on the window seat. He was trying to make himself cool out. He hated his bedroom—all the matching blues and greens, the curtains and the bedspread. Even the twenties movie print on the wall had been chosen because it went with the color scheme. It was all so orderly. Daily, Denis tried to mess things up. He took apart his stereo and fiddled with it, leaving hunks of wire and solder and tools scattered on the Chinese rug. But all he had to do was leave the house for half an hour and the maid would clean it up for him—make things all neat and tidy as if he hadn't ever really been there. It made him feel as if he didn't really exist.

He heard the banging of closet doors and the clicking of high heels from the other end of the hall. His parents were getting ready for dinner out and then that party at the Lawrences'. At least they hadn't asked him to make a showing. Denis let out a sound that was between a hiss and a chuckle. In the past his parents had periodically dragged him along to events like this, just to prove to everyone what an adorable, promising son they had. But since Denis had been suspended from school—twice in one month—Mom and Dad were trying their best to keep him under wraps. The last thing they wanted was for the word to get out that Deann and Steven Daniels, the all American TV Mom and her ideal executive husband, had a problem teenager. Oh, dear. Oh, no.

Denis heard the footsteps get closer. Now he could make out voices.

". . . make sure that he doesn't pull any more crap like that. That Dr. Sullivan is watching for him. We should just take away the keys to his car."

"Steven," his mother reasoned in her famous peppy voice, "just leave Denis alone and he'll figure it out by himself. It's just a stage. Come on, darling, it's time to go. The Douglases are waiting for us at Ma Maison."

"Great," Denis's father grumbled. "Just leave Denis alone, but I'm the one who has to make sure nothing gets in the papers. I think he needs a little old-fashioned . . ."

Denis couldn't stand listening anymore. He put the Talking Heads on the stereo and turned the volume up to eight. The sound bounced in his brain, blocking out everything else. He began to dance like the lead singer in the Talking Heads video, the one in the huge suit. When he looked over at his doorway he noticed that his father had just walked in. Denis kept on dancing.

Steven Daniels scowled. He marched over to

the stereo and turned it off. Denis collapsed on the bed. Mr. Daniels pulled his shirtcuffs from under his powder-blue tuxedo jacket and looked disgustedly at his son. "What are you going to do tonight?" he said in an acid voice.

"Hang out," said Denis, picking up his drumsticks and pounding a rhythm on the bedspread.

Now his mother entered the doorway. In her yellow silk dress and spunky pageboy she looked like an overaged sorority girl. She smiled her famous adorable smile.

"I'd better not hear about any more trouble," Denis's father threatened.

Deann came up behind him, her arm over her husband's shoulder. "Darling, he'll be fine. Won't you, sweetheart?" Denis didn't answer. "Well, I'm sure you will be," Deann insisted. "Helga will make dinner for you. Then she's going out too. We'll be home late. Bye-bye."

Denis watched her cheerful exit. She was always cheerful. No matter what happened she said it was going to be fine. His mother had always gotten by on her sunny smile, while her hired lackies cleaned up the messes. Denis couldn't help wondering how big a mess it would take to make her realize that not everything could be cleaned up.

His father lingered. He looked down at the stereo preamp that Denis had been tinkering with, electronic guts and wires spilling out on the rug. Steven Daniels moved it aside with his Gucci loafer.

"I mentioned you to Cynthia Dickason," he said

in a somewhat more sympathetic voice. Ms. Dickason was one of the directors of his mother's television show. "She said she'd be glad to talk to you anytime, give you advice on getting started. She even said she'd let you sit in the control booth with her. But you have to call her and make a date. It's up to you." He started to get up. "Do me a favor and stay home tonight."

Denis didn't respond. He just kept drumming, harder and harder, even after his father was gone. He didn't stop until he heard the front door shut and the electronic gate open, the Jaguar taking his parents away.

"I'm going crazy," he finally swore to himself. Closing his eyes, he leaned back against the wall. His father was always trying to get him to talk to successful people, as if there were no question that Denis was going to be an executive or an entertainment lawyer or something like that. Like when he'd been chosen to direct a video for media class. That was one of the few times his father had been proud of him, and look what had happened. He hadn't been able to handle the pressure and had been caught for drugs and suspended.

What Denis thought he really wanted to do was work in a recording studio—not as the head engineer or the producer like his father, but just as one of the sound men. He had done that in video class—worked sound—and he was good at it. He liked being in the background just worrying about one thing, not too much attention or pressure. But no, his father wanted him to run a studio or write his own television series. Anything less just wasn't good enough for the son of Steven and Deann Daniels. Ha! Who were they fooling? They didn't want him to succeed for his own sake. They wanted him to make it because his success would be a reflection on them. His parents wanted their real life image to be as perfect as his mother's television show image. And that's what killed him.

He wanted to tell his parents how he felt. But they never stuck around long enough to listen. His mother was always too concerned with her own career, and his father just worried how everything looked. Sometimes Denis thought his parents wouldn't care what he did as long as it didn't interfere with their famous lives.

Denis pounded the bed with his fist. He hated thinking about this stuff, but now he couldn't get it out of his mind. He wanted to forget, to drive so fast or get so loaded that he wouldn't have to worry about anything. He wanted conscious thought to be impossible.

Picking up the turquoise phone, Denis tried to remember how to reach Zee. Zee was a fifteen-year-old runaway who lived in Hollywood with her boyfriend, Kyle. Denis had met them late one night at the Roxy, one of the rock clubs up on Sunset Boulevard. Zee and Kyle always had drugs or booze ... whatever you needed. Denis had written down their number on the back of a concert ticket stub. He opened his wallet and began to look for it.

He had just found it when his telephone rang.

"Yeah?" Denis answered. He smoothed his blond hair away from his eyes with the heel of his palm.

"Denis?"

Denis couldn't believe it when he heard the voice. Nadia. Would she never get off his case?

"Lawrence. What's going on, man? You desperate for a date for your parents' party?" Denis said as rudely as possible.

It took a moment for Nadia to respond. "Oh, Denis" —she sneered—"you don't want to come here. It's going to be too dull, just our parents—you know."

"Don't worry." Denis dangled his soldering iron from the tips of his fingers. He never failed to be amazed at Nadia's ego, as if he were dying to go to her house and see more of his father. "So, Nadia, what do you want?" He was in no mood to be charming, and he knew that Nadia Lawrence wouldn't call him without a good reason.

"Well, excuse me for calling," she huffed. "I just thought you might want to know that there's a very hot party at Kristin Sullivan's tonight just down the street from you. I hear it's going to be very wild and I didn't want you to be left out."

"Yeah, well, if it's so hot, why are you telling me?" Denis asked in a suspicious tone.

"Look, you can take it or leave it. You probably wouldn't know a good party even if you came to one."

"Yeah, well, you can . . ."

Nadia had hung up the phone. Denis hit the bedspread with his fist and then collapsed. So why had she told him about the party? What was she possibly thinking? Confused, he stared at the phone and then back at the phone number of Zee and Kyle.

Nadia. She always had something up her sleeve. She had gotten the better of him before, but he had usually ended up with the last laugh.

Dialing Zee's Hollywood number, Denis began to smile. Who cared why Nadia wanted him to know about the party that pretty new girl was throwing? It wasn't important. What mattered was that he get out of the house, find something to make him forget. Denis stored away the info about Kristin's party and waited for Zee to answer. There was a long night ahead. He would think about Kristin's party later.

❀ 15

THIRTY-FIVE PEOPLE CROUCHED BEHIND THE SULLIVANS' LIVing room furniture. Lights were off, giggles muffled, breath held, as they heard the knock on the front door. Kristin was next to the window looking over her shoulder through a tiny opening in the drape. "Okay, get ready. They're here!" she whispered frantically. More stifled giggles and shushes. Kristin gestured for everyone to stay down as she opened the door. Her heart was racing.

"Hi." She tried to sound surprised. Grady looked at her strangely. He knew her well enough to sense that something was up.

Eddie the showman stepped in. He was wearing a fifties bowling shirt with "Have a Rootbeer" embroidered over the pocket. "Glad you're home," he bluffed easily. "I wanted to get my library ..."

"SURPRISE!!!"

Sound seemed to bounce off every corner, balloons bubbled up, the lights came on illuminating a Dayglo "Happy Eighteenth Grady" banner.

For a moment Grady's handsome face was a

total blank. Then a wonderful transformation took place. His eyes lit up with all the old humor and mischief, and his features came to life. He took off his favorite "Indiana Jones" hat and threw it as high as he could, until it ricocheted off the ceiling and landed in Josh's lap. Grady began to laugh.

"I don't believe this!" he cried happily, looking around at all his friends. His expression became sweetly sentimental. "Thanks, you guys."

There was another raucous cheer, and the crowd broke into small groups, each joking and congratulating the other on the success of the surprise. Grady turned to Kristin and put his hands on her shoulders. His intense blue eyes studied her face.

"Surprised?" she asked teasingly.

"I sure am."

Kristin wrapped her arms around him and moved in close, standing on her tiptoes to nestle her cheek in the warm crook of his neck. He slipped his hands around her waist. "I love you," she heard him say.

Stunned, Kristin relaxed her hold and looked into his eyes. He had said it so softly that she wasn't positive she had heard right. He had never said "I love you" to her before. The people, the room, the party around them, fell away. Only Grady's beautiful face remained clear.

A second later Eddie came over and broke the spell. "Hey, Legs, where's the stereo? I brought everything from salsa to Doris Day." He held an armful of albums, having just ducked back out to the car to get them. Kristin kissed Grady quickly on the lips and turned to Eddie.

"What would we do without you, Eddie?" she laughed.

Grady stepped forward and patted his friend on the back. "What would I do without all of you?" he said. He looked very, very happy.

Eddie was singing along with an old Frank Sinatra record and everyone was laughing, but Kristin and Grady barely heard them. Out on the back patio, they were only aware of the starry sky, the smell of freshly cut grass, and each other. They sat on the edge of the concrete deck, leaning toward each other with their legs intertwined, hands held. In her light drop-waist cotton dress, Kristin could feel the warm breeze down her bare arms and along her neck.

"It's ridiculous to get so crazy about this whole Yale thing, isn't it?" Grady said softly.

Kristin smiled and nudged him with her head. "What do you mean?" she teased. "Your life probably will be over if you have to stay here and go to UCLA instead. It'll be terrible. You'll have to see more of your awful friends, who hate you so much. . . ."

Grady put his hand to his heart in a melodramatic gesture. "That's right, and then there's that crazy girl from Minnesota. What about her?"

"Well, I don't know. She is kind of sneaky. Planning this terrible party for you."

Grady playfully reached around her neck and pulled her in. "I'm so glad you did this for me," he said intently. "Knowing that everybody cared this much, it just makes me feel like it's silly to be afraid. I mean, whether I get into Yale or go to UCLA, I think basically I've just freaked out about graduating and wondering what's going to happen to me—to us. In a way I want to go back east and have all these new experiences." He hesitated and looked at her longingly. "And in a way I don't want anything to change."

"Things will always change. If nothing changed, I never would have moved here and met you."

Even under the dim porch light Kristin could see Grady's eyes soften as he leaned in to kiss her. Her limbs felt airy and light as Grady's warmth encircled her and they slid down till they were half on the patio, half on the grass.

"I love you," she heard him say between kisses. This time she was sure he'd said it.

"I love you too," she breathed.

The kissing grew deeper and more intense, their bodies clinging so closely together that she could feel his heart beating. Under the moonlit sky, it was all warmth and quick breath, and smooth, soft skin. Kristin folded herself against him, wanting Grady, wanting to be as close to him as she could. For a while she was aware of nothing else.

At first she wasn't sure she heard the voice at all. But when Grady pulled away and looked up Kristin saw her too. Elena Santiago, Eddie's sister and a junior at Sunset High, stood looking down at them. Tall, with long, dark hair and a strong slim figure, she looked embarrassed.

"Hi, guys. Sorry to break things up, but I think you should come inside. You have a few uninvited guests."

"Who?" Kristin asked, struggling to smooth her hair and straighten her dress.

Elena shrugged. "I don't know. At least I think they're uninvited. I hope they are."

Clutching Grady's arm, Kristin followed Elena back inside. As she opened the back door Kristin heard a strange kind of laughter—drunken, off balance. When she looked inside, she felt sick.

Four people that Kristin had never seen before were in the middle of her living room—a young-looking girl with half-shaved punk hair and count-less earrings, two boys, probably brothers, in dirty tee-shirts and heavy motorcycle boots, and an older, twentyish guy who was smoking a ciga-rette. He dropped ashes carelessly on the floor as he stood watching them with his hands folded over his chest. He was the only visitor who looked at all coherent. Most of Grady's friends stood around the side of the room, shocked and mo-mentarily intimidated. Elena rushed over to help Josh hold the arm of one of the brothers. They tried to maneuver him back toward the front door.

"I'm really sorry, Kristin," Josh apologized, wip-ing beads of sweat off his forehead. "The front door was unlocked and they just came in."

Kristin stormed up to the guy with the ciga-rette, Grady following her protectively. "This is my house," she said angrily. "I don't know who you are, but would you please take your friends and leave."

The guy gave her an insolent look. He had a

straggly goatee and dark, greasy hair. "No reason to get so uptight. We just came to party."

"Well, then, no problem. The four of you can leave and start your own party," Grady interrupted. Then he grabbed the older guy by the sleeve. "Out, right now."

"Hey," objected the older brother. He was so loaded his legs kept bending underneath him. "Zee said we should come." He gestured to the punked-out girl. "She and Denis said this was one very hot party...." He laughed drunkenly and fell to one side. Eddie deftly removed a pair of porcelain candlesticks from a nearby end table just in time to prevent them from being knocked to the floor.

Kristin didn't know what to do. The last thing she had expected was that these sleazy kids would crash the party. How had they known about it? She was picturing her parents' arrival at a totally trashed house when she saw another unstable figure stumble out of the kitchen. This person she recognized—Denis Daniels.

Denis's eyes were red and unfocused, and his golden blond hair hung in stringy bunches. His wrinkled Oxford cloth shirt was practically unbuttoned and hung over his slender hips. When he saw Kristin he smiled and jolted toward her. Grady stopped him.

"You're Kristin Sullivan," Denis mumbled. "I'm Denis Daniels and we sort of know each other." He let out a high-pitched giggle and tried to put his arm around her. Grady held him back, but not before she smelled the alcohol on his breath. "I think you're nice. You know that," he moaned. "Mmm, good-looking too."

Grady looked like he was going to kill Denis. But Kristin motioned him to stay under control. Something about Denis was so incredibly sad it almost made her cry.

"HEY!"

Kristin turned around. The first brother had broken away from Josh and Elena and had begun dancing across the living room. When Kristin saw where his bulky form was headed, she gasped. He was off balance, prancing toward her mother's glass china closet—the one full of antique plates!

Eddie, John Shephard, and Monica slipped in front of the cabinet, guarding it as if they were goalies at a hockey game. But disaster was only a short shove away. Another group rallied to one side as the boy's large body swerved, hitting the side of the cabinet, for a moment making all the dishes rattle.

Suddenly the boy came to his senses and held out his thick hands.

"All right," he defended, "it's cool. If you don't want me here, I'll go. It's cool." He started to back out, taking Zee and his brother with him. On his way he knocked over a brass lamp. A moment later Josh and three others roughly escorted the older fellow out the door too.

Kristin fell onto the couch as she heard a rusty engine start up. Tires screeched and the car pulled away.

"They're gone," announced Elena.

Trembling, Kristin looked around the living room.

Everything seemed messed up, but in one piece. Then she saw him, and everyone's eyes followed her astonished gaze. Curled up in a corner of the couch, Denis Daniels lay, snoring away like an exhausted little boy.

"Is he okay?" Kristin asked, hurrying over to the sofa. "Maybe we should take him to the hospital or something."

"Don't worry," Elena reassured her. "He's just drunk and went to sleep. He didn't take any drugs—I asked him. In fact, we've just had quite a nice chat. I never knew Denis was so talkative." Elena rolled her eyes.

"What do you want to do?" Grady asked Kristin, his arm around her. "I don't feel right about leaving him here. He might wake up on his own in a little while, but on the other hand, he could stay passed out until morning." Grady frowned. "Somehow, I don't think having breakfast with Denis would be much fun for you."

Most of the party guests wandered away to give them privacy, but Eddie and Josh stayed close. Monica lingered too, a few feet away at the end of the couch.

Kristin thought for a moment. "Maybe we should take him home. He only lives up the block."

Eddie made a face. "We'd better sneak him in somehow. His parents will have a fit, and if I know them, they'll blame us."

Grady looked thoughtful. "Wait a minute. Maybe we should make sure his folks know what's going on. They've been trying to pretend that Denis is

Mr. Perfect since we were in seventh grade. He just keeps getting worse."

Kristin remembered her own visit with Mr. Daniels. She looked down again at Denis, who now looked almost so innocent. She felt sorry for him. He needed help. "You're right. I'll call them."

Eddie got the number for her from Karen Small, who had grown up with Denis. But when Kristin dialed, an answering service picked up. As she was trying to decide what kind of message to leave, Monica slipped onto the sofa beside her. Placing her slender hand on Kristin's wrist, she said, "Hang up. I'm sure they won't be home for a while. They're at that party at Nadia's."

Kristin looked back to the lump on the floor that was Denis. Grady sat down on her other side.

"Come on, Legs," he said. "We'd better just go over to the Lawrences' and tell his parents what's going on. They can come back here and get him."

"Okay."

"No," Monica interjected. "I'll go."

"What?" asked Kristin, confused.

"I'll go to the Lawrences' to talk to Denis's parents," Monica repeated.

"It's okay. We'll do it."

Monica shook her head firmly and stood up. Her dark hair framed her face and her large eyes were set. "No. It's your birthday. You stay here. Besides, I know the Daniels, and I was supposed to be at that party anyway. It's this big Hollywood thing, and it might be hard to get in if your name isn't on a list. It's better if I go."

Kristin looked up at her. Monica's face was

filled with determination. "Okay," Kristin said, "if you really want to."

Monica nodded silently. She took two steps toward the door when a voice stopped her.

"Can I come with you?"

"No, I can handle ..." Suddenly Monica stopped and turned back to the speaker.

"I'd really like to come ... if it's okay," Joshua repeated.

There was a glimmer in Monica's eye and then she smiled shyly. "I'd like that."

As if no one else were in the room, Josh walked up to her and took her hand. Together they walked slowly out into the street.

❋ 16

THE UNIFORMED ATTENDANT OPENED THE DOOR TO JOSH'S green van, and the couple climbed out. Josh stared as the attendant took his place behind the steering wheel, gunned the motor, and drove the van away. "Don't worry. He'll take good care of it," Monica reassured him. She scanned the Lawrences' driveway, which was lined with Rolls-Royces and Mercedes. She realized that the attendant was taking the van to a less conspicuous location.

Josh smiled. He hadn't smiled at her since that day at the beach. Monica felt a wave of warmth.

"He probably wants to take it for a joy ride." Josh raised his eyebrows jokingly and put a reassuring arm on her shoulder.

"Probably." Monica managed a tiny laugh.

Josh stood very close to her. She came just up to his shoulder. "Ready?"

Monica nodded breathlessly.

"Why don't you point out Denis's father and I'll talk to him. You're up for that TV show. You don't want to ruin your chance," Josh offered.

"No." Monica looked down. "This is something I want to do by myself."

"Are you sure?"

"Uh-huh."

Josh lightly touched her cheek. "Okay. Just let me know if you want me to help."

"I will." Together they walked up to the front entrance.

The door was guarded by an unctuous man in an ill-fitting tuxedo. Holding an official guest list, he peered up with a starched, phony smile. But as soon as he saw Josh—who was still in his walking shorts and corduroy shirt—and suspendered Monica, his expression changed.

"May I help you?" he questioned them in a pseudo-British accent.

Monica looked him right in the eye. "Monica Miller. I'm with Rosalind Miller, and this is my escort."

He looked down at his list and, failing to find a reason not to let them in, allowed the couple to pass.

"They act as if we're going to see the queen," Josh whispered as they went into the entry hall.

"You are. There she is." Monica flicked her head toward the far end of the enormous baby-blue living room. There was Nadia, stunningly decked out in a low-cut metallic gold evening gown. She was holding court with a small group of Sunset students and handsome young actors. Glennie and her boyfriend were gathered around too, and one look told Monica that Nadia's party was a triumph. Monica was relieved to see Nadia

take the arm of one of the young men and
drift out to the backyard. Her followers trailed
faithfully.

Glancing around, she saw that the party was in
full swing. The enormous room was packed with
women in full-length gowns or sequined minis
that exposed yards of tanned flesh and real dia-
monds. The big french door at one end of the
living room opened up onto a tented backyard.
Outside was a string quartet, temporary dance
floor, and an enormous table weighed down with
exotic food. Monica could just make out piles of
shrimp on one end and something that she suspected was caviar at the other.

Inside the living room, the party had broken
into clumps. It was a pattern Monica recognized
from other adult Hollywood parties. People drew
together to discuss deals, make pitches for this
part or that writer, and generally "do business."
Those standing by themselves watched the room
carefully, waiting for the right moment to join in.
The smiles were quick and the glasses were frequently refilled.

Passing the bar, Monica had a flurry of nerves
and looked back for Josh. He was right behind
her, his face proud and curious. He seemed in no
way bothered by the fact that they were obviously underdressed and did not belong. When
she caught his eye he held her gaze for a moment
and then winked at her. She felt reassured, her
courage restored.

Finally she spotted Denis's father. She recognized him right away from her audition for "Lau-

rie and Me." He sat on the piano bench—his tux the exact blue of the baby grand piano—next to singer Melissa Manchester, who was plunking out a tune for him and laughing. Deann Lawrence was just behind, humming and holding a champagne glass. Monica took a deep breath and waited for him to look her way.

Eventually he picked her out of the crowd. "Monica! Hi, kid!" said Daniels affectionately.

That was when the woman next to Deann Daniels spun around. Previously hidden by a potted palm, Rosalind Miller took a step forward and stared at her daughter with a shocked expression. Her eyes ran up and down Monica's outfit, finally landing on Josh. There Mrs. Miller's gaze remained, and her elegant mouth fell open.

Monica almost folded when she saw her mother, but she held on to the side of the piano and stood firm. Daniels got up and put his arm around Monica. She could smell the liquor on his breath.

"Now, this little girl," he announced drunkenly to everyone around him—two of the neighboring clumps broke up to pay attention, "this little girl is very talented. She and I may be working together someday." He turned to his audience, for the moment forgetting Monica. "This new series we're doing is going to be real quality TV. I predict it will be almost as popular as Deann's show." He laughed and pointed to another man. "And you know I don't say things like that very often."

"Mr. Daniels," Monica said softly, "can I talk to you alone about something?"

Daniels held out his arms for everyone's attention. "Monica, you're not supposed to do this," he teased, wagging a finger. "Didn't your mother tell you?" He gave her an affectionate, fatherly look. "Honey, we haven't decided yet who's going to do the show, but you are still . . ."

"No, Mr. Daniels, that's not what I wanted to talk about." They were still the focus of everyone's attention. Monica wished they all would go back to their own business. She moved in to Mr. Daniels and tried to be subtle. "It's no big deal. I just need one second. Honest."

"Monica, you're just going to have to tell me right here." Steven Daniels took a fresh drink from one of the waiters. "I'm having much too good a time to leave this piano bench."

There were now at least ten people surrounding them, including the star of a TV series whose name Monica could not remember.

Monica was starting to sweat. "Well, uh, you see Mr. Daniels, it's about Denis. . . ."

His drink made contact with the piano with a nervous clang. His face fell, but he quickly stuck a smile back on. Monica glanced at her mother. Mrs. Miller put her hand to her forehead and turned away as if she couldn't bear to watch.

Monica tried to smile. "So maybe we can just go into the kitchen. . . ."

Daniels looked back at his famous wife. "Why?" His eyes were now daring Monica to cross him. "I forgot that you go to school with Denis," he bluffed. "He's something, isn't he? I hope he hasn't broken your heart. There's nothing I can do about that." Everyone laughed.

Monica felt hot all over. She thought about dropping the whole thing and running out. But then she felt Josh's hand give hers a reassuring squeeze. There was something important at stake here, and they both knew she had to prove to herself that she could do it.

"Denis is having some trouble." She hesitated. Mr. Daniels threatened her with his eyes, but she continued. "There's a party at Kristin Sullivan's, down the street from you, and, um ... Denis is passed out. We would have taken him home, but nobody was there and ..."

Steven Daniels's tan turned a deadly gray.

"He needs help...."

Denis's father stood up, grabbed his wife's arm, and made a quick exit. Suddenly the whole group, including Monica's mother, shunned Monica and Josh. It was as if in the last thirty seconds the two of them had turned into lepers.

"Come on, Monica," urged Josh. "We can take Denis back ourselves and sit with him until he's okay." It was clear that he couldn't stand watching her go through this self-imposed test any longer. He looked at her lovingly. "Let's go."

Monica glanced at her mother one last time. Mrs. Miller's back was turned, but Monica could see the stunned anger in her posture. Taking Josh's hand, Monica headed for the front door. The butler gave them an "I thought so" look as they made their speedy getaway. As they stood outside, waiting for the attendant to deliver Josh's van, they were met by Mr. and Mrs. Daniels.

"We're going over there to get him," Mr. Daniels said, pulling on a white silk aviator scarf. He sounded furious, but kept his voice low, very aware of who might be watching. "I don't ever want to see you for any of my shows again." The Daniels' Jaguar pulled up and, with a slam and a screech, was gone.

Monica and Josh turned to each other.

"You okay?" Josh asked softly, taking her hand.

"Yes," Monica answered, her head held high.

Quietly they waited for the old van, then climbed in and drove away.

For a long time they did not speak, just listened to one of Josh's tapes—a soaring combination of piano and flute—as Josh drove down toward Wilshire.

"Let's stop here," Monica said suddenly, spotting a lovely neighborhood playground. Josh obeyed, making a sharp turn, pulling the van into the small parking lot.

Monica opened her door and hopped down. Tossing off her shoes, she ran toward the jungle gym. The sand felt cool under her feet, and she began to climb. She was so glad to be away from the oppressive opulence of the Lawrence party. Leaning backward, Monica swung her knees from a bar of the jungle gym.

"Does everything look better from upside down?" Josh asked, climbing up to sit across from her. Monica pulled herself up. The light slanted across Josh's face, but she could see his sensitive eyes, the strong line of his cheek. "Monica," he said finally, "do you think Denis's father really meant that, about not giving you a part in any of his shows?"

"Maybe. But he probably said it because he knew I wasn't going to get the part anyway." She laughed ironically. "Honest. If he knew I was going to be his new star, he would have forced himself to be nicer. That's the way it works."

"Weird," said Josh.

"You're telling me."

They laughed. Both kicked their feet against the bars until Josh reached out and touched her leg with his toe. For a moment their eyes met. A cool breeze wafted by, and Monica tilted her head, enjoying the wind through her short hair. She felt freed.

Josh leaned toward her. "I know that wasn't an easy thing for you to do, to face Mr. Daniels like that ... when there was so much at stake.... I guess I just want to say that I think what you did was really brave."

"Thanks." Monica took a deep breath. "You know, it's strange. I just did everything I was not supposed to do—for my career and all—and I feel better than I have in weeks. It feels good to do what *I* think is right. It's so easy to get caught up in my acting to the extent that it's all I think about. I don't want to be like that."

Josh just gazed at her, smiling. "Want to go on the swing?" he asked.

Monica didn't answer. Suddenly, she had so much energy, she didn't know what to do with herself. Josh's presence made her feel so warm and alive. She felt excited in a new way. As quickly as she could she scampered down, grabbing the bars until she leapt onto the sand. Josh was right behind her. Monica scooted over and sat on the swing.

Instead of sitting down next to her, Josh came up behind and gave her a push. He guided her higher and higher. Feeling the air against her face, Monica kicked and pumped her feet for more height, more speed. Josh stopped pushing and watched her from the front. When she got so high that she was almost level with the top of the swing frame, Monica stopped pumping. She let herself slow down, her feet almost scraping the sand until she hopped out, propelled forward. She flew right into Josh's arms.

At first she was laughing, the thrill of the leap still in her. But as she felt Josh hold her and pull her tighter to him, she grew quiet ... absorbing his strength, his warmth. They stood there in the middle of the playground, holding each other for several minutes.

"Monica," he said finally. His voice was breathy and uneven. "I really care about you."

Monica looked up at him. Her heart was pounding like crazy. "Can we just start over now? You and me? Forget all that stuff that happened before?"

Josh thought for a moment, his expression playful. "I guess I can if you can."

Monica was about to reply when he got a different look in his eyes, dreamy and soft. It knocked every thought out of her head. Slowly they came together for their first kiss. Then Josh kissed her again, a longer one this time. Monica's heart was skipping so fast that she had to rest her head against his chest. She entwined her arms around his waist and hugged hard. He smoothed the back of her hair, lightly kissing the top of her head.

"Monica?"

"Hmmm."

Josh gave her a serious look. "Do you know what you're going to say to your mom? She seemed really upset."

Monica buried her face against him. "I don't know yet. We had such an awful fight."

"Are you going to try to talk to her, explain how you feel?"

"I guess I have to. It's going to be hard."

Josh held her tighter.

"It can't be any worse than advanced biology," Josh teased.

Monica pulled back to look him in the face, but he leaned in to kiss her instead.

❀ 17

IT WAS VERY LATE WHEN MONICA GOT HOME, BUT SHE KNEW immediately that her mother was still up. The kitchen was brightly lit, and as Monica walked up to the front door she could see her mother's silhouette through the wooden blinds.

"Good night," she whispered to Josh. She kissed him and looked back toward the window. Josh held on to her hands.

"I'll call you tomorrow morning," he promised. "I'm going over to Kristin's to help her clean up."

"I'll come too."

Monica knew she was just stalling, desperate to stay a moment longer with Josh and postpone the meeting with her mother.

"You'd better go in." Josh gestured toward the kitchen with his head. Gently he took her face between his hands and kissed her again.

Monica watched Josh walk back to the curb; then she opened the door and went in.

"Monica, I've been waiting for you," her mother said from the kitchen.

Monica came in and sat down across from her
mother, a white teapot and a vase of flowers
between them. The high-tech kitchen suddenly
seemed cold and formal, with its spotless tile
floor, white metal cabinets, and wire mesh shelves.
Her mother tapped her nails against her cup—the
only sound in the quiet house. She wore a cotton
bathrobe and no makeup. Her eyes looked tired
and glassy.

Monica folded her hands on the white tabletop.
"I know you're upset about what happened, but I
just had to . . ." She stopped and looked at her
mother, then she tried again. "I'm sorry if I disappointed you but—"

"Oh, Monica," her mother interrupted, "I'm not
disappointed in you."

There was a strange catch in her voice, and
suddenly Monica realized that her mother had
been crying. She couldn't remember ever having
seen her mother cry, and the realization sent a
chill through her.

"I've been thinking."

"About what, Mom?"

Mrs. Miller tightened her grasp around the white
teacup. She looked off and smiled ironically. "About
Denis."

"Denis Daniels?"

"Yes."

"Why?"

Her mother put her hand on top of Monica's.
"Because I see all the problems that he's having. . . ." She stopped to take a breath, finding it
hard to speak. "Because of the way his parents

push him so hard, and then when he acts up they refuse to deal with it. I see it in other kids around here too. I just don't want that to happen to you." Her voice cracked, and the tears began to roll down her cheeks.

Monica stared, amazed to see the transformation in her mother, who had always been so determined, so tough. The tears began running down her own cheeks, and she got up to wrap her arms around her mother. "I'm not like Denis, Mom. I never will be."

Her mother turned and smoothed Monica's dark bangs away from her face.

"I know. But I have pushed you too hard. I guess I sometimes feel like success is the only thing there is. But I know that's not true. Look at the Daniels. They have all the success in the world, and I wouldn't change places with them for anything."

"I know."

"I just get so scared that you'll be all alone like I was, and I want you to be able to get along."

"Oh, Mom. I'll get along. And I'm not alone. I have friends who care about me. If I can just trust them, they'll be there for me when I need them. And I have you."

Mrs. Miller cried harder. "I don't mean to hurt you. I just want what's best for you."

"I know." Monica handed her mother a napkin. Mrs. Miller pressed it to her eyes. "And I appreciate all the help you give me with my career. I guess I just have to do it my own way."

"You'll always have my help," her mother vowed.

She smiled. "Maybe sometimes more than you want, but ..." She looked down and caught a line of tears with her hand. "I just love you so much."

Monica threw her arms around her mother's neck, and they hugged each other. "I love you, Mom," she said.

Monica and her mom stayed up a while longer, drinking hot milk and talking. When Monica finally went to bed, she was exhausted and her eyes were puffy and sore from crying. But the moment she hit the pillow, she slept as soundly and peacefully as a child.

The next morning the whole group met at Kristin's for a massive cleanup before her parents came home. There was a lot of work to do. Dishes were still piled in the kitchen; crumbs from potato chips and pretzels were spread across the carpet. The sound system that Eddie had set up for the party had to be dismantled, and there was still the random mess that Denis and his friends had left. During the evening one of them had managed to dump over a large bowl of guacamole. There was a green splotch on the carpet that Kristin wasn't sure would come out with anything less than professional cleaning. She tried to imagine what she could tell her parents if it didn't come out—that she and Monica had indulged in an avocado fight?

"Somebody want to bring that pail of suds over here?" Monica called out.

"Yeah, and I could use a step ladder."

"I'll get it," Josh replied. He got up from his

knees, rolling up the wires he had disconnected from the stereo speakers. As he passed Monica he paused to lightly touch her hair.

Both of them cracked up as Eddie interrupted, trying to sweep Monica's head with his feather duster. But then they all froze. There was the sound of keys turning in the lock of the front door and it swung open. Kristin's little brother, Shawn, poked his head through.

"Kristin," he yelled out, "we're home. Mom and Dad want . . ." He stopped and stared at everyone and all the cleaning gear. His red hair looked almost yellow in contrast to the sunburn on his face. "Wow," he said, "am I in the right house?"

Kristin came forward and tensed. "Hi. You're so early." She looked back at the crew. They all stared, waiting for her move. "I thought you were coming home this afternoon."

"It was overcast at the beach," Shawn explained, still staring. "Hi, Grady." He looked very puzzled, especially at the sight of Eddie with his dustmop.

"Hello, Kristin?" Mrs. Sullivan said as she came through the door, carrying several bags. Her eyes got large when she saw the group. "Well, hello," she said in a controlled but amazed tone. "What's going on here?"

"Well, uh . . ." Kristin hemmed nervously as she saw her father walk in next.

He put down his bags and surveyed the group. Then he noticed the guacamole mashed into the rug. He slowly walked over and examined it. "Would you mind telling me what's going on?"

Kristin sat down and told her parents everything as best she could. Grady and Josh pitched in with the details of the surprise and Josh's brothers' measles and how and why the party had happened. Dr. and Mrs. Sullivan listened attentively, both faces skeptical and unsure. Finally Eddie and Monica explained about what had happened with Denis.

"Interesting," commented Dr. Sullivan. He scratched his head, his face unreadable.

"So then we had to go over and get Mr. and Mrs. Daniels to take Denis home," she quickly continued.

Josh cut in. "We had no idea he was going to ..."

"Wait a minute." Dr. Sullivan held up a hand. "Are you telling me that you got the Daniels to come over here and pick up their drunken son?"

Josh and Monica looked at each other and nodded.

"They actually did that?" Kristin's father leaned back and began to laugh.

Kristin and her friends exchanged glances.

"In that case," Dr. Sullivan said, still laughing, "you're off the hook. If you kids could get the Daniels to take responsibility for that son of theirs, you're forgiven for this." He paused and looked down at the carpet. "By the way, what is that?"

"Don't worry. I'll clean it up," Kristin insisted.

Her father tried to look stern. "You bet you will. And you will never do something like this again." But he couldn't help breaking into laughter again. "I just wish I could have been here," he said wistfully, "to see that guy come get his kid!"

An hour later the whole house had been cleaned up—even the guacamole spot. Monica and Josh sprawled on the front lawn, lounging in the hot sun. Josh rested on his side and looked up at Monica, who sat cross-legged.

"So she really understood?" he asked, dropping a few blades of grass on her knees.

"Yeah. She really did. As awful as it was, I think it was all worth it. I think my mom and I understand each other a lot better now."

He looked down. "Maybe she'll even decide that I'm not such a bum."

Monica laughed. "Don't worry. We talked all about you. She wants to meet you. I think she's kind of embarrassed at how she acted."

Josh sat up. "I guess if I could give you another chance, I could give her one too."

Monica started to laugh. "Thanks a lot." She grabbed him around the shoulders until they both spilled onto the grass. Josh kissed her on the neck, but then dug his hands into her waist and tickled. Monica laughed and rolled out of his grasp, still giggling. As she turned back, so loose and happy, she saw Kristin coming out of the front door.

"I just got the Dr. Sullivan stamp of approval," Kristin yelled. "Grady and Eddie and I are going to get some Chinese food. You want to come?"

Josh and Monica looked at each other.

"Do you want to?" he asked.

Monica cocked her head. "You know what I'd really like to do?"

"What?"

"I'd like to go look at some tide pools," she told him.

Josh hopped up, grinning. "Sounds great to me. Thanks, K," he said, pulling Monica to her feet, "but I think we're going to go off on our own."

Kristin nodded warmly and walked them over to Josh's van. "Where are you going to go?" she asked as they climbed in.

Monica pulled her door shut and leaned on the window frame. "The beach," she said, looking over at Josh. "I have a lot of sand-castle-building to catch up on."

Josh slid a new tape in the old tape deck and waved good-bye. Monica laughed with delight as the two of them cruised toward the Pacific.

Here's a sneak preview of TEMPTATIONS, book three in the continuing "Sunset High" series of books for GIRLS ONLY.

Eddie started to get up, but then sat back down. "Oh, one more thing," he said, as if it was the most casual thought in the world.

"Yes?"

"How'd you like to go to the prom?"

Everything stopped. Eddie tried to smile. Holly just sat there like someone had just told her the earth was really the moon. Her eyes were huge.

"What?" she finally whispered.

"I know it's kind of heavy for a first date and all, but as you said yourself, I'm different."

"Are you serious?"

"Oh, yes."

"Honestly?"

Eddie nodded.

Holly looked down at the table and scraped the empty plate with her fork. For a long time she did that. It was as if she were determining the fate of all civilization. Finally she raised her head. "Okay."

Now it was Eddie who was in shock. "You mean it?" He didn't mean for it to come out quite so hysterical. He stood up, too excited to stay in his chair.

Holly smiled at him, and Eddie felt like he had his arms around her even though they weren't touching at all. At the same moment they both began to laugh. It was as if they were on so much the same wavelength that the impulse hit simultaneously. He felt very close to her.

Just then the Patisserie front door opened and Jeremy stuck his head in. "Holly," he called.

Holly turned. "Yes?"

"The limo's here for you."

Holly glanced back at Eddie. "I have to go. I'll see you at school, okay?"

He sat back down in his chair. "Okay."

Holly got up, gave him one more smile, and she was gone.

Eddie crept up to the front window. He got there in time to see a black-suited chauffeur usher Holly into the back seat of a stretch limo. Eddie scratched his head. He'd felt so close to her, and now he felt so far away.

ABOUT THE AUTHOR

Linda A. Cooney grew up in Southern California and has worked as an actress in both New York and Los Angeles. In addition to creating the SUNSET HIGH series, she has written five other popular young adult novels. She lives in New York City.